LUCIE'S TOMB

Jon Ferguson

Huge Jam
2025

First edition, published by
Huge Jam, Gravenhurst, England

ISBN: 978-1-916604-32-2

ARE NOT THOSE WHO SAY
THEY KNOW THE TRUTH
THE WORLD'S BIGGEST LIARS?

AUTHOR'S NOTE

This book is a work of fiction. There are different voices, all my own, that are in no way intended to be those of other people either living or dead.

Two curious ideas came to mind after I finished the book yesterday. The first is how my obsession with the value of all creatures originates, oddly, in my Christian upbringing. Most Christians (I was raised in the Mormon faith) seem to put man just below God on the totem pole of what counts in this life. The standard hierarchy of value kind of goes like this: God, man, animals (big ones in particular), plants, rocks, etc. It's all sort of micro-waved Platonism. But for whatever reason (perhaps because Jesus was the only Christian I ever really cared about in all the holy books), fifteen years of Sunday School left me thinking that all living creatures should be respected and given equal dignity.

The other oddity is that yesterday was Easter Sunday. After sixty-two years on this earth, I have found no reason to believe that Jesus, or any other creature, has ever been *resurrected.* In this book the dead often say how they are just rotting away to dust. Of course, I'd like nothing more than one big party in heaven with each life going on forever under positive circumstances, but my intellectual conscience won't let me believe something is true just because I might wish for it. I had no plans to finish writing the book on Easter, but ironically, that's what happened.

J. F.
April 9, Morges

LUCIE

1972–1992

CHAPTER 1

The little town of Pully on the shore of Lake Geneva is where I live. I say "live" but it's really more like "half-live". My husband died a year ago and it seems like when he died, half of me went with him. My name is Georgina, I'm Swiss, sixty-seven years old, and I come from a very devout religious family. I tell you this immediately because hatching from such an egg can be like having a bowling ball attached to a foot for the rest of one's life. So, before I go any farther, let me explain what kind of an upbringing I had. I won't mention the specific name of the church my parents – and of course us kids – were a part of, but I suspect one could get a similar education in any number "We-Know-the-Absolute-Truth" groups, like Seventh Day Adventists, Jehovah's Witnesses, Mormons, and so forth. I think mine was a little more extreme than most. But I'll let you be the judge of that.

In my family, at the dinner table, only the adults were allowed to talk. In God's house – church – neither women nor children could open their mouths. Women sat on one side, men on the other, and the men did all the talking. When I think back on it all, it's pretty amazing how all the so-called "prophets" in the world have come up with these wild ideas about men, women, animals, churches, Jesuses, Gods, heavenly and hellish kingdoms, resurrections, salvations, dispensations (I never really knew what a "dispensation" was), good and evil, right and wrong, and you name it, the prophets have spewed it! And not only that, but to think how they got so many millions of innocent (or maybe not so innocent) people to follow them and how these followers had kids and they had kids and they had kids and they all believed in the same stuff! O what a world it is! Anyway, I was one such kid. Fortunately, I met my husband who is now unfortunately in his grave. But the more I think about it, the more it really is incredible how these religions all say that life is a neat package and that all you have to do is take off the ribbon and the wrapping paper (did you see the film "The White Ribbon"?) and inside there is some beautiful black book that has all the answers to the whys and wherefores of everything that happens in existence. What was really a mess for me was that when I became a teenager and started thinking a little for myself, I felt guilty whenever my mind and body were telling me to try new things and think new thoughts! And what really set the house on fire was when I finally stopped believing in the whole circus and got thrown out of the tent. Then, my whole family saw me as some kind of a dirty black sheep, and I got tossed on the other side of the fence for "life"! I really did. How so-called "Christians" can do such a thing, I don't know. Yet they did. I had no family until I met my husband, now deceased, but that is why he meant so much to me when we got married forty years ago. He called himself an "assnostic", which always made me laugh! The only thing he believed in was trying to get by in life with a minimum of pain and suffering ... kind of like a cat, I always thought. But Charles died last year and our two kids left Switzerland a long time ago. My daughter lives in Frankfurt and my son in London. I see them sometimes at Christmas, but now that their children are grown, we rarely get together. Actually, my husband and I had very few friends. I do have one very kind adorable niece that I see from time to time. She left the religion too and lives twenty minutes away in Vevey. Otherwise, I am quite alone.

Our – my – apartment overlooks the Pully cemetery where Charles is buried. As I recall, we got a really good deal on it because a lot of people didn't like the idea of having a view of a burial ground. But we didn't care, and we figured it was better to have a cemetery across the street than a high-rise apartment. Now it's very practical because I just have to walk across the street to visit Charles, and I pretty much go every day. I keep fresh flowers on his plot and always make sure his tombstone is clean. He was a stickler for order and cleanliness. Maybe he didn't believe in God, but like most Swiss, he sure believed in clean toilets and sinks!

Charles and I still have our little conversations. I'll ask him how he slept and he'll answer the way he always did,

"Fine dear, and you?" Then I might tell him that I saw my niece for lunch or that I walked to the store and bought a new light bulb for the kitchen, and how these new, long-lasting, super-duper energy-saving ones are all you can find these days and that they cost ten times more than the old ones used to and how every time I buy one I think I'm wasting my money because they'll probably outlive me! And then Charles will say something like, *"Don't be silly, dear."*

After I see Charles, I often wander all over the cemetery. I like to look at other graves and I check up on some of the people who don't get a lot of visitors or attention. It makes me wonder if being dead can get lonely, too. I often bring extra flowers to place on tombs that never have any, and I'll sometimes sweep dirt off the messy ones so passersby can at least see who's sleeping, hibernating, or rotting away down there. I have one new friend that I especially like talking to, a girl named Lucie who, as far as I know, hasn't had one visitor for the whole year since I've been coming to see Charles. All her grave says is ...

Lucie

1972- 1992

... That's it. No last name. No nothing.

The first time I noticed her was about three months ago. There wasn't a trace of any flowers having been there and the writing on the stone was unreadable because of dirt and weeds. It looked more like a grave for an animal than a person. I had my little broom with me and I cleaned it up spic and span. The next day I put a rose on each side of her name. Actually, these last few days I've been talking to Lucie more than to Charles. We are becoming very good friends. She tells me about her life and I tell her about mine. It's funny because when we talk, I always stare at the five letters of her name and the numbers of the years of her birth and death. I stare so hard that the L, u, c, i, and e don't even look like a name anymore, and I stop seeing the letters and numbers, but only the grey of the stone. Then I start seeing Lucie's face like she's on TV or something. Suddenly she will begin telling me about her baby blue pajamas and how she loves lying in bed and thinking about all the stars in the sky and the animals on the earth. The other day she told me about the time they found their cat dead behind their house, and her stepfather said that it looked like it might have been poisoned, but that they would never know for sure. What's interesting to me is that when I talk to Charles, I know I'm really talking to myself, but when I talk to Lucie it feels like she's really there and that we're two young girls conversing together.

I can't believe it's already December. Charles died on the third of January which means it's been eleven months since he moved across the street into the cemetery. Time doesn't fly, we fly. It hasn't snowed yet, but it'll come soon for sure. When it does, it makes the graveyard look like one big beautiful lumpy bed with a white blanket over it.

CHAPTER 2

It's been a week since I slipped on the ice. It still hurts to walk. I decided not to go to the cemetery today. I haven't left the apartment all day. I had breakfast like always, but instead of going across the street to see Charles and Lucie, I plopped down in my chair in front of the TV. For some reason I didn't turn it on and I really don't know why. I sat there staring at the screen with the remote-control gadget in my hand and I started thinking. One thought after another. I had no idea where they came from, but they came. First, I thought it was pretty crazy how people didn't have TV for a few zillion years and then, all of a sudden, people like me spend half their lives watching other people do things instead of doing things themselves. And they watch people they will never meet in their lives and who don't care a single solitary bit about them! They watch them talk, fight, play, argue, cry, complain, kiss, eat, travel, etc., etc. I suddenly almost felt sick to my stomach thinking about how much time I was wasting. I guess I

wasn't really wasting it because I was occupying myself…
babysitting myself you might say. But that's just it!
MYSELF hardly existed. MYSELF wasn't doing
anything but wasting away like the people across the
street in the cemetery. That's when I really started
thinking … about ME … ME … Georgina Monnier, age
sixty-seven, born in 1944, raised in a prosperous Christian
fundamentalist family in the prosperous conservative
town of Vevey in the prosperous conservative country of
Switzerland in the prosperous conservative heart of
Europe … and now … now … here, a woman alone in a
chair waiting to die, hoping death will unite her with her
husband but not really believing it will … me, a woman
whose days consist of watching a damn TV, visiting a
cemetery across the street, walking to a grocery store up
the street, cooking, eating, cleaning an already clean
apartment, and sleeping. Then getting up the next
morning to do it all over again.

I wondered what Lucie would think. Lucie had twenty
years on this earth. I've had sixty-seven. But maybe she
did far more things in those twenty years than I've done
in my sixty-seven. First, I lived in the Christian world and
everything was God, Jesus, salvation, and sin. When I
think back on it, the guilt and sin part of it really had me.
It felt like I had a razorblade in my chest and everything I
did twisted the blade and cut out a piece of my heart. Then
I met Charles. He helped me climb out of that hole. We
had babies. I watched them grow. Then they flew away
like smoke out of a chimney. Charles died. Here I am in
Pully in my chair front of the TV. But I'm not going to

turn it on. No, I'm not. Not today. Today I'm going to keep thinking…

… I started thinking about the earth, this big ball of water, dirt, and rock that I am riding on. Is it really big? Is it big or little? It had always felt big to me but suddenly it felt very small. I started thinking about the stars and the galaxies Lucie was talking about the other day, and how the earth was just a little itsy-bitsy dot floating around in infinite space. How big is infinity? How small is the smallest bit of life?

Suddenly I liked these thoughts. I closed my eyes and imagined my chair was flying through space. Then I realized I wasn't imagining it – my chair really was flying through space! With me in it! The earth is spinning, moving, flying all the time. It's one great big carnival ride … or great *little* carnival ride! But it's going on all the time, with me on it or not … The earth racing around the sun at a few thousand kilometers per hour. Does it matter how fast it's going? It's going. That's all. Fast and slow. Big and little! What about me? Am I big or little? How many molecules or cells or atoms make up me? Millions … trillions … zillions. Does that make me big? I'm one meter fifty-nine. So what? Everything is small when compared to what's bigger. Everything is big when compared to what's smaller. And what if Georgina Monnier is neither big nor small? And the earth is neither big nor small? If it's all a human invention … all of it … every last millimeter, every last atom!

I suddenly wondered if I was intelligent or stupid. Same problem. And what about this brain stuck in the middle of my head? I didn't ask for either my brain or my head! I didn't plant one inside the other. Haven't both been keeping me locked in a cage all my life? I always had a little trouble with mathematics in school. Just because sometimes I couldn't add 45 to 96 ... so what? Maybe my teachers were the stupid ones for judging me just because my little brain couldn't add up a couple of dumb numbers. I was a nice girl. I never stole a piece of candy. I was never unkind to people. I wanted to be on that golden train to heaven. I tried to be good, but deep down inside I thought I was guilty. Guilty because it was impossible to be good. Only God was good. We were sinners ... rubbish ... human drivel. And then my brain started telling me things like it's telling me now. Things like how all these prophets bellowing about Jesus were nothing but imposters and schemers trying to get followers and make money and be somebodies themselves in this wild crazy world. And do you know what? This is what really got me thinking about these prophets being full of baloney: If there was a real God, why would He or She wait so long until Jesus was born. And then after Jesus died, why would He or She wait until the nineteenth century (that's when our Church got started by our so-called "prophet"!) to bring "the truth" to the poor little world. Why would God not have done this a thousand years ago, or two thousand years ago, or ten million years ago? How can people be so stupid as to believe God would do something like that? And if God created men, why did He or She put such stupid brains in their heads – brains that couldn't add 45 and 96 and couldn't figure out that all the founders of these wild religions were full of double baloney? Why? And to think that all my life I've been thinking about God and Satan and Jesus and sin and heaven and hell simply because I was born in Vevey of parents who believed a charlatan named _____. Had I been born in Tokyo of Shinto parents, my life would have been a completely different story!

Yes Georgina, big-small, right-wrong, tall-short, good-evil … all inventions of the human brain … Go on Georgina … keep talking to yourself. You're having fun. You're feeling light. You're laughing. You haven't laughed like this for a long time. When you were a child, you weren't supposed to laugh. You weren't supposed to have fun. You weren't supposed to talk at the dinner table. And because you were a woman, you weren't supposed to talk in church! But now you're talking. Now you're laughing … Why don't you say a prayer, for old times' sake. Get down on your knees and pray. Oh, but my hip hurts! Okay, then pray in your chair. Sure, why not?

Dear Universe … Please bless this world that there is no god — at least not the kind like the one in the Bible and the fundamentalist religions like the one I was raised in — a god that makes people feel guilty all the time and has everybody judging and arguing and even killing each other, a god that sends people to heaven and hell and has a so-called "savior" show up after a few million or billion years and then sends all these phony prophets to earth to mess up people's lives with all their silly beliefs that make people like me spend their lives in cages feeling lousy about themselves, a god that doesn't make brains big enough or strong enough to set people free to fly through the

cosmos with smiles on their faces. Thank you, Universe, for being sure there is no god like this.
Amen

As soon as I finished my prayer I thought, "What in heaven does *'amen'* mean anyway?" Here's a word that I used for years as a child and adolescent and I have absolutely no idea what it really means or where it came from. Then, for whatever reason, I started thinking about the alphabet itself. Where did *it* come from? A-b-c-d-e-f-g-h-i-j ...Who thought it up? All the way to z. And a–m–e–n? Who invented all these cute little combinations of lines, circles, and curlicues? Who mixed them up and made all the *"words"*? Just mixing up the four letters in "amen" and you can get "name", "mane", and even "mean"! In English anyway!

I don't know how long I sat in my chair with the TV off. But I did. And for the first time in a long time, I actually had fun ... with myself.

CHAPTER 3

Yesterday Lucie told me that she didn't like the shape of her nose and that her legs were too long. I told her she had one of the cutest noses I had ever seen and that her legs were beautiful. "Mon cul!" she said. "I look like a giraffe with an elephant's nose!" We both laughed and then she went on about how one of her favourite things in the whole world was coming home from school to find that her mother had just made a batch of cookies that were still warm and when she took her first bite, she didn't know which she loved more, her mother or the cookie? She also told me that she loved Christmas with her family in the Jura mountains when they went skiing and sledding and sometimes the sky was so blue that she was sure God had painted it for the holidays. But when it was grey it was beautiful too because it made the snow and pine trees look like they were glowing in the dark.

The day before, she had said that she actually started to stop believing in God when her cat would kill a mouse and not even eat it, but would just leave it on the doorstep all bloody and dead. Why would God create a creature that would do that? And why would God let earthquakes and avalanches happen that killed animals and people? Then she changed the subject with a story about when she was ten and the boy next door kissed her so long and hard that she was sure she would get pregnant. She had me laughing so hard I almost fell on her tomb. Needless to say, we're getting closer by the day …

CHAPTER 4

... And today I didn't even go to Charles's tomb, but only to Lucie's. I wanted to talk to her about a few things I knew I couldn't discuss with Charles. First was the subject of love and what it really is. All that thinking about words and the alphabet had got me wondering. I remembered the Beatles song *"All You Need Is Love ... Love ... Love Is All You Need"* and I finally asked myself: *Love ... Do I know what it is? What have I really loved in my life? Did I really love Charles? Do I love my children? Myself? The world? Do I love being alive? If I don't, why not? Should I?* I didn't want to know what Jesus or the milkman loved. I wanted to know what I, Georgina Monnier, loved. I babbled all this to Lucie as I stood there in the cold staring down at her name and the 1972-1992. I was dressed warmly so it didn't matter that she made me wait a bit before answering. I had on wool socks that come up to my knees, my long wool skirt, and the thick black winter coat that Charles bought for me not long after we met. I could feel Lucie thinking.

Too many people talk without thinking. They get asked a question and immediately spit out the answer. But not Lucie. Sometimes I'll ask her a question and she won't say anything for five or ten minutes. Sometimes she'll think a whole day before answering. I guess when you're stuck in a hole in the ground forever and ever, there's no hurry about anything. Anyway, after a few minutes she said, *"Georgina dear,* (I love it when she calls me 'dear'), *love is one of the strangest things in the world. Loving a fruit, a dress, a book, a friend, a song, a movie, or a man are all very different things. There should be different words for all the different kinds of love. But there aren't. It's a perfect example of how poor human language is. To love a fruit, you have to eat it, suck it, chew it, digest it, and then send it into the toilet. To love a dress, you have to wear it over and over and it has to love your neck and shoulders and hips. To love a book, you have to talk to the book and the book has to talk back to you. The pages have to feel like they are glued to your feet and they follow you everywhere you go. To love a song, you have to have the music carried in your blood through your whole body. That's why your spine tingles when the music is just right. To love a movie, you have to be in the movie yourself, in all the characters, not just the lead role. Their voices are your voices. Their joys and tribulations are your joys and tribulations. Loving people is much more complicated because people move, talk, breathe, laugh, cry, believe in things, change, and have values. When you put all those things together, loving another person is the rarest thing and the most wondrous mystery of all."* The tomb went quiet.

I've thought about this for most of the day.

After I left Lucie I went back home, made a cup of tea,

and fell into my chair. I tried to let my mind wander, wander like Charles and I used to do in cities in Europe when we went on our little vacations before the children were born. We would never buy a map. We would take the train to Paris, Venice, or Rome, find a hotel, drop our things on the bed, and then go for a walk. Charles wasn't one to immediately throw me on the bed and start taking my clothes off. No, he wanted to explore the city first. I loved those trips ... Did I say *"loved"*? I did. What did I mean? Go on Georgina – think! How many kinds of love are there? Start counting! First, the Christian idea of *loving thy neighbor as thyself.* A humdinger that got put into my head when I was five years old. At that age it made perfect sense, so I tried to be nice to everybody and never say bad things. I thought I was "loving" people and that I would go to heaven. But I wasn't loving anybody. Being nice to people isn't loving them. I was probably being nice to people so that they would be nice to me and so I'd get to heaven. And then I thought about the idea that we are supposed to love people the way we love ourselves. But this doesn't work because I don't think most people really love themselves. In fact, loving yourself might be even rarer than loving other people. Even my beautiful niece in Vevey tells me she has never loved herself and she is one of the nicest, prettiest, most intelligent people I've ever met. If she doesn't love herself, who does? Not long ago we talked about it and she said she thought she didn't love herself because she believed her father had never loved her. He never said anything nice to her to make her feel good about herself. How sad! A father doesn't love you and you spend your whole life not loving yourself! One man, who probably didn't love himself because he didn't get love from *his* parents, messing up a self-image for *life!* Maybe all you need *is* love ...

Then I started thinking about another problem. Our love is supposed to be universal, but how can you love 7,000,000,000 people? Back in Jesus's day there were probably only a few thousand people running around Jerusalem and Bethlehem, so loving everybody made some kind of sense. But today we know that there are millions and billions of people in China, Russia, America, Africa, Australia, Japan, Indonesia, Europe, Iceland, Greenland ... in every corner of the planet. Back in Jesus's day people had no idea how big the earth was. It almost made sense to love everybody. But today, if I really put my heart into it, I might be able to find time to love everybody in the town of Pully, but any more than that, forget it! But of course, Jesus probably meant just to love "everybody" you bump into on a day-to-day basis. But even then, what does it really mean to "love" people? Does it mean to respect them? To respect their right to live? To respect their right to do stupid things? To respect their right *not* to love people? Should I respect people who don't respect me or others? It surely doesn't mean to love them in the sense of romantic love. I can't be wanting to kiss everybody, sleep with everybody, and make babies with everybody. It doesn't even make sense to want to hug everybody. If I hugged everybody I met on the street, it would take an hour to walk fifty meters! So what did Jesus mean? Probably what I thought about in the first place. Just be nice to people. Don't make their day worse than it already is. Say hello and goodbye with a smile on your face. Don't kick their dog or scratch their car ...

But what about Charles, the man I spent almost four decades with? Did I love Charles? At the beginning I said that when he died, half of me died as well. That was the way I felt then, when I wrote it. But that was before I started thinking, before I started talking with Lucie. Maybe Charles was more of a habit than anything else, an addiction, the drug of my life. When you say hello and goodbye to the same person every morning and evening for forty years, that person has to become a part of you. He could even be your jailer if you were in prison or your master if you were a slave. Charles was caring. Charles was good to me. He was generous. He didn't pee on the toilet seat. He put his dirty socks in the basket ... But did I love him? Did I *really* love him? I do miss him, yes. I missed him immensely the first few months after he died. But is missing somebody proof of love or proof of habit? That's what I'm starting to wonder.

Now I'm starting to have a new routine. Now I have Lucie. A year has jumped in between a living Charles and a dead Charles. Now I'm starting to look in the mirror and wonder who I am or was or will be and if that person has ever truly loved anybody at all! I wonder if I'm actually starting to *think*. Fifty years ago, I doubted my religion. Now I'm starting to doubt my whole life ... *Yes! No! Did I really love Charles?*

One thing is certain: the way I felt about Charles evolved greatly over time. Maybe I should say "changed" instead of "evolved". It didn't evolve in a straight line. It was more of an up and down, in and out, over and under. Sometimes I wanted him. Sometimes I didn't. Sometimes, when I looked at him across the dinner table, my body felt warm and I wanted to reach over and take his hand and kiss him. Sometimes looking at him inspired nothing. Rarely – it did happen once or twice –he disgusted me. On those occasions I now wonder if he disgusted me because of *me*, not because of *him*. Maybe it was because *I* was in a nasty mood that made him look nasty too – like with food when you're sick.

Another thing I ask myself: Why did I take pictures of Charles when he was dead, lying in a coffin like a figure in a wax museum? But I did. I took two dozen of them, from different angles. For some reason I wanted him frozen in time in that coffin. But why? I even gave a couple of the pictures to my niece in Vevey. Why did I want those pictures? Why did I want to guard the memory of Charles lying on his back like a wooden toy soldier, packed into an ugly metallic rectangular box, his nose the highest point of his elongated body, his eyes closed, his hands folded across his mid-section like a good boy in church, his toes pointing toward heaven? I wanted Charles, dressed in his last suit of clothes, dead, going nowhere forever, ready to rot in that coffin until there would be only dust. Why? Why did I want those pictures? I'm not sure. But I wanted them. I took them. At first, I actually thought he was the lucky one because he didn't have to suffer any more on this earth, because he didn't have to feel tired or lonely anymore. Now I've started to change my mind. He has started to look pathetic in that coffin. Death has started to make me sick. Sometimes I feel like a bee trapped in a glass jar knowing that soon my oxygen will run out, knowing that one day I will drop to the bottom of the jar and my wings will never flap again, knowing that I will be in a silly hole in the ground next to Charles and there will be a gravestone saying "Georgina Monnier, 1944 – 20__" and it will get dirty and nobody will sweep it or put flowers on it except maybe my niece in Vevey. I used to look forward to lying in the cemetery with Charles. Not anymore. Now just the thought of it makes me claustrophobic. I don't think I took those pictures to have a final memory. No, I took those pictures in the hope that one day Charles would jump up out of that silly coffin, knock me on the head, and shout, "Georgina, you fool! Live! Live, damn it! Live as much as you can before you end up looking like me!"

Suddenly I had an idea that I've never had before. Where in this universe is it written that you should love somebody for more than five minutes? For more than ten minutes? For more than two days? For more than a month? More than a year? More than ten years? Where did the idea of "eternal love" come from? The only thing that's eternal is eternity itself. Everything inside it changes, swirls, evolves, devolves, melts, meshes, mashes, disappears. Where did this idea of the "perfect partner" come from? People change, everything changes. How in God's name can people expect to "love" each other for forty years? Of course, some people do. Good for them. But so what? Is that what's desirable? Isn't it better maybe to love a bunch of different people over the course of a lifetime? Who wants to eat the same meal every day for forty years? Charles and I stayed together that long. Then he died. I was never unfaithful to him. I never got to know another man deeply. I never became intimate with anybody else. Is that a good thing? Perhaps there was another man out there who would have been a much better match for me than Charles, whom I would have made far happier than I made Charles and who would have made me far happier than Charles did. Had I not been bombarded with Judeo-Christian principles – principles of family, loyalty, infidelity, adultery, sin, hell, fire, and damnation – would I have had a totally different "love life"? Would I be a completely different person today? Would I be sitting here writing what I'm writing, thinking what I'm thinking?

That's enough for today – enough writing and talking to myself.

What will my head say tomorrow?

CHAPTER 5

Georgina went to see her niece, Jana, this morning, the lovely woman in Vevey with twins that were pulled from her mid-section after her bulging belly was slit with a fine surgical blade. Georgina still has a car that she uses from time to time. She drives slowly, but such little trips give her a sense of freedom from her world around the cemetery. The roads were clear of snow and ice. She left a little before ten and took the lake route, a stunning drive in any weather. Today the water glistened, those snow-covered Alps poked the blue sky, and the vineyards on the steep slope to her left were like rows and rows of miniature Giacometti sculptures. She was talking to me most of the way, explaining how beautiful the world can be. When she's happy, I'm happy.

Her niece is really the only other person – besides me – with whom she can talk. And like me, she is a very good listener. But she reveals less of herself than I do. I tell Georgina more or less everything that pops into my head, even if sometimes it's a little fabrication or exaggeration. On the other hand, sometimes I'll stay quiet for a while to give Georgina the feeling that something profound might be brewing in my rotting pile of bones. The niece always seems to be holding things back, as if her mind filters all her thoughts and very few make it to her tongue. She seems to be afraid of how people will take things and certainly doesn't want to make life unpleasant for Georgina. I'll say anything to make Georgina feel good, like that day when I was telling her about the blue pajamas and being so happy with life. That was all just to give her a little joy. I never had any blue pajamas. But it worked. We became friends. She got warm and happy. In any case, from my perspective being truthful went down the drain a long time ago. Words just became toys, or sometimes hammers and nails.

Anyway, Georgina's niece Jana still has a beautiful innocence about her. Though she is very smart, she still thinks there is some kind of meaning and order to the universe. One thing she and I agree on is how lonely Georgina is. And I'd hate to think of where Georgina would be if she hadn't had her niece after Charles died. She really had nobody else to talk to. Fortunately, we found each other as well. Today she bombarded Jana with ideas about love. *Had she loved Charles? Did the Christian ideal of love make any sense? Should one love others as one loves – or doesn't love – oneself? Was every object of love loved in a different way? Was the language of love vacuous, insufficient, or both?* ... Jana had listened attentively, adding small bits of her own ideas here and there, but mostly letting Georgina clear her mind. They'd sat at the dining room table and drank Christmas tea. The niece had placed a plate of delicious sweets between them which Georgina slowly, but surely, emptied. What other sensual pleasures does she have besides food? Without sensual pleasures a person might as well be a rock, a bunch of bones, or a religious fundamentalist who thinks the body is sinful. I couldn't believe it when Georgina first told me that in her family you weren't supposed to laugh, cry, express emotion, or show affection, and that her own her father had been that way. She said that he never expressed love of any kind, except love for a "god" that no soul has ever seen, heard, or touched – a god that only exists in the lines of so-called "sacred" books. What a world! You're supposed to pile love on a fairy tale god in a faraway heaven, but you're *NOT* supposed to show love for the people you live with and associate with every day! What kind of a religion is that? The same religion that says "Love thy neighbour as thyself" tells you *not* to show love for your own family! Of course, all Christians aren't that way, but Georgina swears that's the way things were in her family. Not in mine, that's for sure.

The more Georgina talked, the more I think she was beginning to think that she hadn't really loved Charles that much. She explained to her niece that Charles was a lot like her father, the niece's grandfather. Both men rarely showed any sadness and rarely manifested any joy. (Georgina burst out laughing when she said Charles used to try to muffle his orgasms when they made love!) Charles wasn't a whacko Christian like her father, but he did have that same kind of icy personality. She is starting to think that maybe that's why she married him ...

Before Georgina left her niece's apartment, Jana invited her to come for Christmas Day. A great idea. I didn't want her just standing over mine and Charles's tombs all day. She needs company in the flesh, not just us dead people.

CHAPTER 6

Last night, after spending a wonderful day talking with my niece, I went to the cemetery for the first time after dark. I always go in the morning, but I finally got up the courage to go at night. It was an experience I'll never forget.

There was nobody there. It was a clear crisp night. At first, I wandered slowly, aimlessly. There were candles on many of the graves twinkling like the stars above. They shed a light on the tombstones that made them look like little spaceships. "We're all floating in the depths of outer space," I thought. "We're far out in the middle of nowhere!" And the funny thing was, as I said this I realized – like that day in my chair – that we really *are* out in the middle of nowhere. Here we are, riding along on this little planet in this enormous universe with stars everywhere in every direction, and we *act* like we *know* where we are ... We're "home"! We're "on earth"! And the earth is *near* the moon and the sun! And because of this we feel cozy. Like a baby wrapped in a warm blue blanket! Like Lucie in her blue pajamas! ... But where are we, really? What do we really know about where we are? Nothing! We have no idea where *we are*. We're out in the middle of NOWHERE! All these dead souls around me, these stars and galaxies above and below me, in every direction, dead friends in every direction ... not just Charles and Lucie ... but everybody! We are all in this together – all riding this crazy planet to nowhere!

The funny thing was that I wasn't scared, not a bit. To the contrary. I don't think I've felt so happy for a long time – maybe forever. It was like I was walking on air. Weightless. I was *crazy* happy. The world was crazy, I was crazy, everybody was crazy. But I was happy, happy to be a passenger on this crazy earth! Maybe it only lasted ten seconds. I really don't know. But for the first time in my life, I felt completely insane, completely wild, completely *free*, completely alone but at the same time completely tied to all that was around me, tied to everybody, both dead and alive, every tree, every road, every candle, every star, every blade of grass! Yes, Georgina! You're alive! You're part of the show! Part of the circus of life and death! *Infinitely small ... infinitely big ... Who knows? Who cares? Nobody knows! Nobody cares! It doesn't matter! It's there! It exists! And you're part of it, Georgina! Here! There! Everywhere! Nowhere!*

When I got home, I immediately called my niece. I tried to tell her what I felt, but I didn't explain it very well. How do you explain an orgasm in a cemetery? How do you explain the feeling of being totally lost and totally found at the same time? Of being totally insignificant and the most important creature on earth at the same moment? Of the same head being sane and insane? Of the same heart being empty and full? Of the same person being a genius and an idiot? Of knowing everything and knowing nothing? Of being omnipresent and nonexistent at the same moment?

I asked Jana if she wanted to come with me to the cemetery tomorrow night. She said she'd love to, and asked if she could bring along her twin daughters. I couldn't see any reason to say no. Everybody should see the Pully cemetery after dark.

They're coming at seven-thirty.

This morning, I looked at myself. Not in the mirror of my mind, but in the mirror in the bathroom, the real full-length one on the back of the door. Charles's maroon bathrobe has hung there for twenty years. I left it on the hook intentionally after he died. But today I took it down when I got out of the shower. I decided I wanted to see myself, all of myself. Normally I just look down at my body when I'm naked. I have a quick aerial view. All I can see are two big breasts, a wave of fat, and my toes. Today I wanted the frontal view. The whole thing. And the rear view, too. I wanted to look at my big round sixty-seven-year-old butt. I wanted a look at all one hundred and fifty-nine centimeters of Georgina Monnier. Maybe it was the experience in the cemetery last night that made me fear nothing. Not even looking at myself, closely, in a mirror.

I used Charles's bathrobe to dry off, then I dropped it on the floor. There I was. Me. Every centimeter and kilogram. It must have been the first time I had looked in a mirror in the nude for ten years. Maybe fifteen. Maybe for as long as Charles's bathrobe has hung over the mirror. I stared. I slowly turned sideways and took in the side view. Then I did another quarter turn, craned my neck, and got a glorious view of my double-moon butt. That's what it looked like ... two full moons stuck together like Siamese twins.

Suddenly my eyes felt like they were eight years old. Little Georgina was staring at this strange naked old lady. Little Georgina's eyes bounced from the greying hair to the rounded nose to the thin mouth and sagging chin. Then they slid down the tree-stump neck, stopped between the heavy breasts, wandered across the flabby waist, halted briefly at the grey patch of pubic hair, then slowly trickled down the fat layered thighs and surprisingly slim calves, and finally locked on the chubby wide feet. Then suddenly the eyes popped back up to the face again. Eyes met eyes.

"Look Mommy!" little Georgina said. "Look at that nice fat lady with no clothes on! Is she from the carnival or something? Is she in the circus? How did she get into our bathroom? How did she get in here while I was taking my bath?"

"Well, I don't know," her mommy said. "But the Lord works in strange ways. You know that. Mommy and Daddy have taught you that. The Lord's ways are not man's way. He must have invited this nice lady into our house for a reason. Everything has a reason. I'm sure He wanted to tell us something."

"But I don't think she can talk, Mommy. She's just looking at us like she's some kind of statue or something."

"Why don't you ask her a question or two and see if she can talk?"

"Okay Mommy, I will. *'Hi, I'm Georgina. I'm eight years old and I live in Vevey and this is my mommy. Who are you? Where did you come from? What are you doing in our bathroom?'*"

"A big smile lit up the fat lady's face. Her teeth looked pretty good for an old person. They were almost white. She started moving her lips. At first there was no sound coming out of her mouth, but then, little by little, Mommy and I were able to hear some words. It was like she hadn't talked for a long time and her voice was rusty like an old door that hasn't been opened for years. The words kept coming though. The first thing that I could understand was an 'if'. Then she said a 'you', and then 'don't' ... 'watch' ... 'out' ... 'you'll' ... 'end' ... 'up' ... 'looking' ... 'exactly' ... 'like' ... 'ME!' She started laughing hysterically. She laughed so hard I thought she might fall on the floor. But she didn't. She finally stopped and looked at me. Her face completely changed. Her head tilted to one side. Her eyes were gentle like a dog's. She timidly extended her hands toward me. I took two steps forward and put my hands in hers. 'Do you want to know a secret?' she whispered. 'I'm going to tell you a secret, little Georgina.' She squeezed my fingers. 'For the first time in my life I love myself. Today. Here. Just now. With you looking at me. Your eyes told me they loved me and they transmitted your love to me. Thank you. Thank you, my dear. Thank you so much.' She let go of my hands and I stepped back next to Mommy. We looked at each other silently for a moment and finally the fat lady said, 'It's taken me sixty-seven years to fall in love with myself. I hope it doesn't take you that long!' Then she winked at my mommy and started laughing again. I don't think I've ever seen anybody so happy in my whole life. At least nobody in my family!"

CHAPTER 7

I almost hit my damn skull on the lid of the coffin when I saw how happy Georgina was standing there naked in her bathroom. She was still happy – and a little out of breath – when she came over to tell me about it.

"Lucie! Lucie! You won't believe what just happened to me!"

"Yes, I will. I believe everything that happens. Nothing in this world surprises me anymore."

"I've been alive for sixty-seven years. You know that. And for the first time in my life, I *like* myself. I really like myself! After my shower, I was standing in front of the mirror staring ... at myself. I hadn't done so for years."

I didn't tell her I already knew all this. Like always, I let her tell her story.

"All of a sudden, I thought: 'Holy Jesus Mageesus! I'm alive! Who cares if I'm not the most beautiful fish in the pond? Who cares if I'm not the most intelligent kid in the school? Who cares if I'm not rich or famous and have a double-moon for buttocks? I'm alive! I'm not dead! I can breathe, eat, sleep, feel, touch, walk, drive, talk ... Hell, I could probably still make love if I could find the right bull!"

"Now you're talking," I said.

"So, I immediately got dressed, put on my overcoat, gloves, and hat and went for a walk all over Pully. I walked down to the lake and looked at the swans and ducks. I can't believe they're still here in the winter. But they are. Then I walked up into town through the old part of the village. I looked at the vineyards. They even made me want to have a glass of wine. Then I walked up the hill to the forest. I looked at the pine trees pointing up at the sky. I thought of how deep their roots must be to keep them upright, to keep them from falling down in strong winds. Then I thought of my roots, my dogmatic Christian roots, my stern father's roots, my do-what-God-says-or-you'll-go-to-hell roots ... and I thought ... *Well, at least they kept me standing for sixty-seven years!* Suddenly I wasn't mad anymore. I saw all the roots of all the world. I saw everybody from the beginning of time and their roots. The world was one big tangle of roots. I kept walking through the forest and thinking. Thoughts were shooting through me like bullets through a machinegun. I thought I can't blame my father for being who he was. I can't blame the phony prophets for being who they are. I can't blame Jesus or Paul or Moses or God or the devil or the wind or the rain or the earthquake or the snake or the spider or the condor of death that swoops down and steals the baby from its crib. Suddenly everything looked innocent. And the thought of me standing naked in front of the mirror an hour earlier almost brought me to tears. 'Georgina, you fool!' I thought. 'You've been so cruel to yourself. You've been nice to everybody else all your life, but you've been unkind to yourself. You were taught not to judge others and you didn't judge others. But you judged yourself. You said you were not loveable. Not even loveable to yourself. That was your only sin. It wasn't quitting your religion. It wasn't not believing in the Bible and God and Jesus any more. It wasn't letting Charles into your bed before wedlock ... No, your only sin was not loving yourself!'"

Then Georgina started to cry. Her tears fell like drops of rain on my tombstone. They covered my name; they formed a little stream that curled down to the years of my birth and death. For someone who had been taught to hold everything inside, she had really learned how to let it all flow out. I think all the joy and sadness of her life was lying in that puddle of tears. I felt it freeze to solid ice not long after she went back home.

CHAPTER 8

My niece's twin daughters are called Julie and Isabelle. You can't really tell them apart except that one has a little bump on the end of her nose. That's Isabelle. She must have been squished in the corner in the uterus against her sister's knee. Otherwise, the two look exactly alike. They're the happiest kids on earth, but their personalities are very different. Julie is a little shy and mysterious. Isabelle is funny and outgoing. Julie can be funny too, but it takes time to get her out of her shell. Isabelle was never in a shell. They're kind of like the yin and the yang. I imagine them in that position in utero. They rarely fight or argue, but when they do you can tell it's just a game and that they're never really mad at each other. I think they got that from my niece. She is good to everybody. She's probably the most "Christian" person in the family, yet she's the one everybody imagines will go to hell because she thinks all the founders of Christian sects are quacks and that the Christian god is no more real than the Hindu gods or the Aztec or Mayan gods. If there is a God and He, She, or It is a decent creature, if anybody will go to heaven it's Jana. She spends almost all her time helping other people, including me. I try to tell her she should think about herself, but, at the same time, she has helped me more than anybody else.

They're coming over in an hour for our nighttime visit to the cemetery. It's another cold clear evening. There are no clouds to blanket the little town of Pully tonight. I just called my niece and told her to be sure they all wear lots of sweaters, scarves, and jackets. "Bundle up," I said. "The stars aren't giving off any heat tonight."

Before they come, I want to quickly tell you about the conversation I had with Lucie this morning. She asked me to explain a bit more about my father and how he (like his father) never showed any emotion. She can't understand why these people were – are– like that. What can be the reason for not wanting to express love, joy, sadness, or even anger? What kind of a God give us emotions if we were not supposed to convey them? I told her these people are convinced that this life is a test. Nothing else. You pass the test, you've got your ticket to heaven; you fail and you get fried like a chicken on a grill. You're not on this earth to have any fun. You're here to show God that only *GOD* matters. Lucie asked me why a God would want people to spend their lives worshipping Him. She said that sounded like an extremely self-centered god. I told her she was right. Then we talked about what she thought the purpose of life was. She believes it has no purpose and that's why it's so incredible and fantastic. She thinks it's sad that people who give life "a purpose" have a tendency to shut out all the other things that are *not* part of that purpose, and that not only do fundamentalist types do this, but all kinds of people do it ... parents do it, schools do it, politicians do it, culture does it, lawmakers do it, philosophers do it, fashion does it, even Buddhists do it – why wear orange robes all your life when you could also wear brown, pink, green, red, yellow, white, purple, and every colour in the rainbow? When I asked her how she got to be so smart in only twenty years of living, she said she didn't consider herself smart, just open-minded. That's when I said she reminded me of my niece, but the difference was that Lucie was probably born into a family that opened up the world for her, whereas my niece was born into a totally hermetic world where everything was black or white, prohibited by God or ordered by God, good or evil, right or wrong, and she – at a young age – had to break down the walls, question everything she had been taught, and slowly forge her own vision, her own values, her own good and bad, and her own ideas about what and who to love on this earth, what and who and *how* to love in a universe void of sense, void of higher meaning, and void of supreme justice, heavenly redemption, or a divine hand that saves some and damns others. Lucie got a little excited by the conversation. It almost sounded like she was kicking the coffin with her feet. Of course, I explained how I left the religion too, but I did it much later in life and I had Charles to hold my hand and help pull me away. My niece did it all on her own starting at age sixteen and while she was still living at home. Lucie said she was looking forward to meeting Jana and that surely one day – not tonight because the daughters were coming – the three of them would talk about it all at greater length.

The doorbell rings.

Hello Jana. Hello Isabelle and Julie. It's always so nice to see you.

Hi Aunt Georgina.

It's good you're all bundled up. It feels like Swiss Siberia out there, doesn't it? Well, let's go now and then we'll come back here and have some tea or hot chocolate. Let me get my coat and hat.

She puts on her bulky black coat and wool hat. They leave the apartment and walk across the street to the entrance of the cemetery. The gate is always left open until ten. The church bell up the street chimes seven-thirty. There is light from the moon and, to a lesser extent, from the candles on some of the tombs. There are fewer candles than Jana expected. Julie and Isabelle run ahead.

Girls, come here! Let me show you something … Here. This is General Guisan's tomb. He was the most famous Swiss general.

I thought William Tell was the most famous general…

General Guisan was a general during World War II. He was born here in Pully.

You could fit twenty people in his grave!

C.F. Ramuz is buried here, too.

Who's he?

I've told you a little about him. Don't you remember … the famous Swiss writer.

Oh yeah, I remember, Mommy. He wrote books about

walking in the mountains and kissing pretty girls! Where is he, Aunt Georgina?

Just down here. Come this way.

The girls skip ahead down the middle of the cemetery. They have no fear of the dead or the living.

Your daughters are so adorable.

They're the perfect age. Nine is perfect. They're still children. Their bodies are still little girl bodies. They have only just started looking in the mirror.

You were a happy girl too, Jana. In spite of everything.

I spent a lot of time alone. Where is Ramuz's tomb?

Just over here to the left.

It is very pretty with the candles on the graves.

And tonight we have the moon ... Here's Ramuz's grave ... Girls! Come over here!

It's very simple. It's rather the opposite of General Guisan's.

Julie and Isabelle, this is where C. F. Ramuz is buried.

Where's Uncle Charles, Aunt Georgina?

This way. He's not far. I've brought some candles, so we can each set one on his tombstone.

They walk less than thirty meters.

Here he is.

Georgina takes the candles and a box of matches out of her bag. Charles's grave is decorated.

Let me just show you where my friend Lucie is.

Who's Lucie, Aunt Georgina?

She's a girl I found a few months ago. She had no friends so I befriended her.

How can you make friends with somebody who's dead?

You can, if you try. She died very young. When she was

twenty.

How did she die?

I don't know, but I suspect one day she'll tell me ... Here she is.

Aunt Georgina, doesn't she have a last name? It just says "Lucie".

That's cool ... like soccer players. Daddy always talks about Pelé, KaKa, and ... what was that other guy's name?

So, Lucie was born in 1972 and died in 1992 ...

I hope I don't die when I'm twenty.

But grandma says that after this life there's a much better one in heaven with God and Jesus and angels and stuff ...

Girls, I don't think anybody really knows what happens after we die. We would all like to know of course. But I'm not sure anybody really does. You will make your own decisions about these things when you get older.

Georgina takes a candle from her bag. She gives it to Isabelle and hands the matches to Julie. Julie lights the candle and Isabelle kneels and says, "It's for you Lucie. Goodnight."

Georgina doesn't take them to the corner of the cemetery where the infants and small children are buried. They go back to the apartment for a warm drink.

Jana and the twins are home in Vevey at half past nine.

CHAPTER 9

What really strikes me sometimes is how most people never grow up. Separating children and adults is a joke. When does the child become something other than a child? It's surely not at a certain age. An eighteenth birthday isn't going to change anything in a person's character. Just look at Georgina. She's still a child, a wonderful child, an intelligent child. But she's a child … an innocent child. When I saw her with Jana's children, I thought: "There's no difference between Georgina and those girls. Just age, but age itself doesn't mean anything. I love Georgina with all my heart, but the truth is, I love her like a child. And there's nothing wrong with that. But I swear she never grew up … or maybe I should say she never had a chance to grow up. She was stuck in her conservative frigid world, then Charles took her away and slowly she found herself in a placid new world with a husband, two children, and an apartment. But she was really "playing house" like children play house. I'm not saying that such is a bad thing. No, not at all. But it's true that most people "never grow up".

Look at the things adults believe in and the things that are important in their lives. They're just like kids' beliefs and kids' toys, just a little bigger and more complex. Kids have teddy bears and dolls, doll houses and tree houses, tricycles and guns. Adults have husbands and wives, big houses if they can afford them, fancy cars and weapons that can really kill. Kids believe in the Easter Bunny and Santa Claus. Adults believe in God and justice and political parties ...

Life is one long continuum. There is no moment when a child becomes a man or a woman. Menstruation and pubic hair are no guarantee of anything except increased sexual excitement. Menstruation and pubic hair don't make the mind a more refined observer of the world and the intricacies, complexities, causes, and effects of what goes on in this universe. They are no guarantee of "adulthood". Most people basically stay on the same train tracks from crib to coffin. Of course, Georgina has gone through many changes. But children go through changes. Adolescents go through changes. Old folks go through changes. But what really makes a child an adult? Not change itself, but a certain kind of change, a change in the way one perceives and reacts and understands, a change in the way one views oneself and one's relation to the world one was brought up in. One must create some distance; one must step out, step away from the herd, and with one's own wings fly above and look at the world as one circles the sky. Then maybe one has a chance to be a "grown up" person.

I think Georgina's niece might have taken this path. I think she might be someone who has "become an adult", who has "started to write her *own book*". I don't know her well enough yet. But I'm going to keep my eye on her. Of course it's not too late for Georgina. It's never too late. It's just that most people don't have the tools to pry open the prison door and step out into some fresh air.

From where I am I have the luxury of observation: lots of time, lots of inverted space, lots of eyes: time to think, space to occupy, eyes to see farther than the limits of culture and language.

I think I'll sleep for a while now. It's been a rather long day.

CHAPTER 10

O Lucie, O Lucie ... when I see my niece's daughters, I can't help but compare their childhood with mine. And I was raised in the same house that they live in; I climbed the same stairs to go to bed every night; I brushed my teeth in the same basin; I sat in the same dining room and was not allowed to say a word during meals until I was ... how old? I can't even remember ... maybe thirteen or fourteen. Their mother is so cheerful around them and so kind. She smiles, plays, laughs. She pushes no religious dogmas down their throats. She just wants them to grow up with a certain intelligence to allow them an open view of life and the world. She just wants them equipped to live the life they choose in the best way possible.

And me ... my childhood ... my bedtime stories were verses from the Bible. Usually not the verses about Jesus loving all his sheep, but the verses about sin, hell, fire, and damnation. I was afraid to do anything as a child except sit like a zombie and do as I was told. I was afraid to laugh, to cry, to run and shout with other children. I was afraid to speak to adults. I didn't sing, except the songs in church about salvation and meeting God and Jesus on the other side of the veil, once this life of misery was over. I didn't dance. Dancing was a sin. I waited for my parents to choose my husband (for whatever reason, they never did). I went to school. I did my homework. I was a good student. But I wasn't learning for myself. It was for my parents, my teachers, God, Jesus, and the angels above. For everybody except myself. I never learned for the simple beauty and curiosity of learning. I learned so my parents wouldn't scold me at home if I got a bad mark. I learned so if I never found a husband to take care of me, at least I could have a job that would keep me in food and lodging. I never read books for the pleasure of exploring new worlds and meeting new people. The world was not to be explored. The world was evil and sinful and unclean. I was to be protected from the world. I was not allowed to see television. I was not allowed to read books that would sully my mind, books like "Jane Eyre" or "Wuthering Heights", books that all girls should read. I wasn't allowed to go to the cinema with my friends. When I went to bed at night the only thoughts I was supposed to have were about God and Jesus. I was not supposed to be thinking about the boy behind me in school or the dress I saw in the shop window around the corner ...

That was my life. And when I think of my niece's daughters' lives, the lives of Julie and Isabelle, I imagine what my life could have been.

I know, dear Lucie, I know I should not dwell on the past. You've told me before. I know I should only think of what life I have left before me. But's it's hard. So hard. The other night in the cemetery when I watched the girls skip from grave to grave, like they were playing hopscotch, I couldn't help but imagine if it *had been my mother there and not Jana. My mother would have made me walk next to her, in silence, with my arms down and my hands clasped behind my back. Like a prisoner. Like a slave. Like a punished child going to a dark damp room. But Julie and Isabelle had fun at the cemetery. They danced under the chandelier of the moon, they ran from candle to candle, from grave to grave, like children playing games at a birthday party. They were not thinking about death or heaven or duty to some phony prophet's perverse version of God. They were thinking about life, this life. And they were enjoying it. I'm just beginning to understand what it might mean to enjoy life.*

Lucie remained mute though my whole soliloquy. If she said something, she didn't say it loud enough for me to catch it. She's like that sometimes. She knows when I need to talk.

Then I went over to see Charles. I have been neglecting him. Though it was only four o'clock, I put a candle on his grave. He thanked me, then began talking about the first Christmas we spent together:

Remember dear, we had that little hotel room in Les Paccots, the quaint ski village near Châtel St. Denis. You were pregnant with Nicolas and had not been feeling well for a couple of months. Let's go away for Christmas, I said. And we went to Paccots for three nights. When we got there, there wasn't a flake of snow on the ground in the village and only a little on the mountains above. I had my old 2m10 Rossinal skis and wanted to ski. You said you didn't feel like skiing even though the doctor had said it would be okay as long as you were careful. We walked around the village and I bought you some chocolates. Do you remember? – black chocolates in the shape of Christmas trees. You always liked dark chocolate. Then we went to a café for coffee. We sat next to the window and looked at passers-by. We began talking about how we would raise Nicolas – of course at that time we didn't know if it was a boy or girl. You said love was the most important thing. I said it was giving the child guidelines and strong principles. Like what? you asked. Oh, honesty and hard work, I said. You put your hand across the table and I covered it with mine. While we were talking a few isolated snowflakes started dropping to the ground. They looked like they were in slow motion. That night it snowed fifty centimeters. When we woke up the blacktop streets and concrete sidewalks were transformed into a winter wonderland. In the afternoon I skied while you rested in the room. I remember when I came back you were asleep on the bed with all your clothes on. I kissed you and wanted to make love, but you said you weren't feeling well. I remember the dinner we had, veal and rosti. I drank a little wine, but you didn't because of the baby. You were always cautious. At midnight we were still awake – you had slept all afternoon while I skied – and we went to the mass in the church in the middle of the village. We thanked God for each other and our child, but God doesn't exist.

I stood there, waiting for Charles to say something more. It had been his turn for a little monologue. But he had finished. He said nothing more. It's so nice to have someone to listen when you need to talk.

Tomorrow is the twenty-fourth of December. I'll be alone except for Lucie and Charles. But I am invited to my niece's home for Christmas Day.

CHAPTER 11

Maybe today I'll tell Georgina a few new things about my life. Maybe I'll invent a few things, put a little frosting on the cake. It all depends on how she's feeling. I might even talk about my death. No, it's too early for that. All I really want is to see her suck a little joy out of the rest of her life. What else could I want for her? Sometimes I feel like I'm Georgina's damn long-lost recently-found prophet trying to lead her to a tiny promised land as her candle of life slowly burns down. If I have to tell a few lies along the way, it'll be worth it … Speaking of candles, Christmas Eve is always the night when the greatest number burn in the cemetery. They do create an atmosphere, sad for some, joyful for others.

Georgina didn't come until around six o'clock. She likes the candles in the dark. As expected, I had no other visitors during the day in spite of all the traffic in my vicinity. It is amusing how the whole neighborhood vibrates at Christmas time.

Good evening, Lucie.

I waited while she set a candle next to my "e" like she always does.

Hi Georgina, and for whatever it's worth … Merry Christmas.

You too.

Have you seen Charles?

Not yet. I spent some time with him yesterday. He was more talkative than usual and I was more of a listener than is my habit. I'll take him a candle later. I wanted to see you first.

And I've been looking forward to your visit.

We exchanged a few banalities. She said she was anxious to go to her niece's the next day. I told her that meeting her had been the highlight of my year. When she asked me if any members of my family had come to see me today, I told her no, but explained that that didn't mean they didn't care. I said we just had different ways of doing things than most people.

What does your family consist of? she asked.

My parents and a sister. My father is really my stepfather. My real father went to Australia when I was two years old. I don't remember him at all. As far as I know he's still there. My sister is three years older than me.

Does she remember him?

Hardly at all. Our stepfather raised us. She was five when our real father left. She says she only has a vague memory of him washing a car in the driveway and squirting water on her. We lived in Pully, down the street by the lake in a small house.

Were you born in Pully?

Well, you know there's no hospital in Pully. But I was born in Lausanne. I always lived in Pully though.

What kind of house did you have?

It was quaint with a small garden. My sister and I each had our own bedroom.

Are your parents still there?

No, after I died, they moved to the Italian part of Switzerland. I don't know where exactly.

And your sister? Where is she?

I'm not sure, but I think she's in Australia …

This was the truth. I sensed Georgina was a bit concerned. I decided to change the subject back to my stepfather.

My father – my stepfather – was a musician. He played the piano. As far as I know he never made the big time, but I think he was quite close to being a top soloist. He didn't like to promote himself. By nature, he wasn't the ambitious type. He was a bit shy and reserved. He played a few concertos with the Orchestre Suisse Romande, but he made most of his money giving lessons at home in our house. Ines – my sister – and I saw him give a few concerts. The only one I really remember was when he played Rachmaninoff's 3rd Piano Concerto in Victoria Hall in Geneva. I'll never forget the look on his face when it was over. It was like he was empty, drained, dead … like he could hardly stand up to take a bow. We were on the second row. It turned out it was his last public concert. I never knew why.

How old were you?

Probably twelve or thirteen.

So, he taught you and Ines to play?

Ines yes. Me just a little. She still plays, I think.

Georgina was staring very hard at my tombstone. She

had that look on her face that always told me that she was thinking very fast. Finally she said,

You weren't interested in music, Lucie?

Yes, of course I was, to an extent. But I was more interested in books. My mother was an avid reader and very smart. She used to read all day, mostly the classics, in English and French ... "Jane Eyre", "The Grapes of Wrath", "The Brothers Karamazov", "The Magic Mountain", "Anna Karenina", "Madame Bovary", Hemingway, Shakespeare, Stendhal, George Elliot ... I remember because as soon as I was eleven or twelve, she started passing some of them on to me. I read quite a few, especially the ones about women. I think that was her way of educating me. She let the books do it. By the time I was fifteen I felt like I had lived ten lives, but in fact I had lived nothing. That's when my life really started ...

I paused. Before Georgina said anything I went back to talking about my mother.

My mother abhorred housework ... vacuuming, washing windows or clothes, sweeping, mopping, changing sheets, ironing and all that. In this she was very unlike many – or most – Swiss housewives who seem to take great pride in a clean organized house. Not my mother. She hated it with a passion. She was a wonderful cook, however. When she wasn't reading books, she had her nose in a recipe or a frying pan. She and my father both loved food. This too they passed on to Ines and me.

Did your mother "mother" you as a child? Did she pamper you?

No. She wasn't the type. She put us in the world, gave us a start, and then kind of said "good luck", rather the way deer raise their babies and then leave them in the wild. She rarely played

games with us or took us out to buy clothes. It wasn't that she didn't care, but more like her idea of life wasn't raising children. I think she gave us a lot of freedom because she liked us out of the house, out of her hair, so she could have the peace to do what she wanted. She was not a bad mother by any means. To the contrary, I'm grateful for the freedom I had. She did, however, have a very melancholy, depressive side. Sometimes if the weather was bad and we were all in the house together for an extended period of time, she would suddenly snap at us for no reason ... at my stepfather, too. In retrospect, I think these moments came from the fact that she felt boxed in. She was like a tiger in a cage that was just a little too small. She didn't mind so much being in a cage, but the cage she was in just wasn't quite big enough. I think had she had just one child she would have been happier. But two ...? Maybe if we had had more money and she could have travelled more, that might have helped. But we – or they– rarely went to Paris or Venice or London, places my mother talked of often. She had spent two years in London as a jeune fille au pair and she spoke perfect English. As a girl, I know she had seen Italy and she often said how she loved Paris.

Did your parents love each other? I don't mean to pry, but ...

Georgina, you know you can ask me anything. I enjoy nothing more than talking to you.

Thank you, Lucie. I feel the same ...

Did they love each other? That's a complicated question in most cases and my parents were no exception. I think they did, at least in the beginning. But by the time I was old enough to observe things, they rarely showed each other any affection.

I don't think my parents were ever in love.

I know. You've told me ...

Neither of us spoke for a few seconds. Finally, I said ...

You must be getting cold standing out here.

Not really. I have my long underwear on, and my mittens. I'm fine. Do you know why your real father left when you were young?

Not exactly. My guess is that my mother had fallen in love with my stepfather and didn't love him anymore. But I have absolutely no memory of him and my mother never spoke about him.

You said your life started at age fifteen. How is that? What do you mean?

What do you think, Georgina? What happens to girls at fifteen ... ? They fall in love ...

I didn't.

That's because of that strict education of yours. My parents were the opposite. I think they were happy to see me go from being a little girl to a woman in a few months' time. I didn't get my period until I was fourteen. And the next year I'm living Anna Karenina and Count Vronsky. Actually, it was more like Jane Eyre and Rochester. He was much older than I was.

Did your parents mind?

Not my stepfather ... my mother somewhat ... maybe ...

Were you beautiful, Lucie? Don't be modest.

People said I was. Actually, I think my mother was both proud and jealous. Not so much jealous of me, but jealous of the passion she observed, but didn't live.

How did you meet the man?

Oh ... umm ... he was one of my father's students. He came to the house twice a week in the afternoon for lessons. My father really liked him and as he was ... uh ... the last student of the day, my father would often invite him to stay for a drink. I would be home from school and I'd sit in the living room with them. We would laugh, joke, talk about everything and nothing. He was from Canada and he had a great sense of humor. He loved to tell stories.

So, what happened? You fell in love. Did he?

Absolutely. Sometimes I think he loved me more than I loved him. He was so passionate. He often said that love is so hard to find and that to waste it was a crime against humanity ... or something like that. We waited until I was sixteen before we made love. It wasn't easy, but it was worth the wait. It was "illegal" until then, but at sixteen only my parents could denounce him. Actually, they were the ones who told us it was okay. Well, my mother did. She knew we were in love and one day she took David ... that was his name ... into the kitchen and said, "David, we know you and Lucie love each other. We want you to know that everything's okay. We have no objection to your relationship. Just be sure you take the necessary measures to ensure that she doesn't get pregnant." So, we had the green light and let me tell you, we ran through every intersection possible. We must have made love five hundred times that first year.

I don't think Charles and I made love more than two dozen times in our thirty-eight years of marriage. At least I know I didn't. Maybe he did when I wasn't looking ... And the rest of your relationship?

We played, laughed, joked, walked. At first, he didn't have a car and we'd take a lot of walks along the lake. When he finally bought this old beat-up Volkswagen Beetle, we often went to the mountains. When he had a little money, we'd drive around

France and Italy.

So, he was your first love. Were you his?

No. I think he had had a couple of lovers before me. But he didn't talk about them much.

Were you really happy together?

Oh yes, Georgina, we were. Especially the first two years. It was the happiest I think I ever was in my life ... Well, maybe that's not true. When I was a little girl, I was happy because I didn't have a care in the world. But that's a different kind of happiness. With David, I shared the world and we shared our bodies. It was a beautiful exchange ...

Suddenly I choked up a little. I don't know if Georgina noticed it. I coughed a couple of times.

It's a beautiful story, Lucie.

Yes ... was all I could say.

Neither of us spoke until I finally told Georgina that I was tired. I thanked her for coming and for listening. We wished each other a happy Christmas. She said she would go see Charles. I said I would go back to rotting in my stinking grave ... No, I didn't say that. But I wanted to.

CHAPTER 12

Charles actually seemed to be waiting for me. He knew what day it was. I think he was surprised I came so late ... maybe "surprised" isn't the word; "hurt" might be closer to the truth. I didn't get there until a little after six. I wondered how he could be hurt at this stage of the game, but I didn't say anything.

Hello dear. It's me. Merry Christmas.

Merry Christmas Georgina.

There were quite a few people in the area. I knew he wanted to ask me where I had been. But he didn't. Instead, we reminisced about our Christmases over the years: when the children were young and waiting for Santa Claus; the time it snowed all day on Christmas Day and in the afternoon (there were no cars on the streets as it was impossible to drive) we sledded from the apartment all the way down to the lake; when Charles got some kind of food poisoning and threw up all night; the Christmas when Santa Claus gave Nicolas his first bicycle and he learned to ride in the living room because it was too cold to go outside; when our youngest, Lydia, had croup so bad that we had to take her to the emergency room at the hospital and I slept there with her for two nights, so Charles and Nicolas had a "men only" holiday.

We talked a lot, but I could tell Charles was in a melancholy mood. I had come to him happy because of everything Lucie had told me. Now I was slipping back with Charles into a flattened-out feeling, a feeling that happiness is like an orange – it is much easier to press out the juice than put it back in.

Sometimes I wonder if reminiscing is a bad thing. What do you do? You think about old times that will never be again and you end up feeling sad. You end up feeling like somebody dug a hole in your gut and didn't fill it up. You end up wishing you were places where you aren't. But on the other hand, reminiscing can make you feel fortunate, fortunate to have at least had the happy moments you have had, fortunate to be alive and have been alive, fortunate to have had something rather than nothing.

In any case, I stayed with Charles for a good while. I held his hand (so to speak) and tried to leave him in a state of reasonable contentment, but wondering if contentment was really ever the lot of man. Before leaving I put two candles on his headstone. Then I hurried home to have a cup of tea. I turned on the television. I don't watch the stupid box nearly as much as I used to, but sometimes it is like a warm blanket that makes certain chills go away. I mean really, who watches TV on Christmas Eve except the loneliest of the lonely? But I'm not in that category ...

Tomorrow, I go to Jana's house. It's always a place I like to go. And when I think I was raised in that house! I spent nineteen years in that house! Sometimes I wonder if my parents didn't find me a husband because they wanted to keep me there forever. In many families of my parents' religion, the last child – particularly the last daughter – is expected to stay in the home and take care of the parents as they age. I was the youngest and it would have been my job to babysit my mother and father until they died. By that time, I would have been too old to find a husband. At age twenty, when my parents were not yet sixty, I went to Bern where I got a job as a translator. Three years later I married Charles. I adeptly avoided my "duty".

I don't know if I've told you that Charles had already been married twice before he married me. At the time I didn't know if it was a good sign or a bad sign: it might have been good in that he hadn't found the perfect mate and I was to be it; or it might have been bad if he had been impossible to live with and two women prior to me had booted him from their homes. It turns out that neither was the case. I definitely wasn't Charles's Aphrodite and he was not an unpleasant person to live with. He was actually very easy to live with: he made the bed; he didn't leave his clothes all over the floor; he wasn't a picky eater; he would help with the cooking and washing up; he wasn't mean to the children (he wasn't a whole lot of fun either); he never yelled at me and rarely at the children; his snoring was tolerable; he showered regularly and hardly ever released an unpleasant body odour; his sexual appetite was minimal which was all the better for me as I was never able to shake off the part of my religious education which hammered into my young brain the absolute unshakable idea that the human body was *not a toy to be used for sensual pleasure!*

Yes, Charles was not unpleasant. But was he pleasant? Sometimes I think it was as if I spent thirty-eight years with a roomful of bland furniture, or as if I had lived with a large blow-up doll in the shape of a man ... He never hurt me, but he never brought me any real joy. I'm not trying to be cruel. Not at all. I'm just trying – finally– to figure out who Georgina Monnier really is and what her life is all about.

CHAPTER 13

I must admit that I can't disagree with anything Georgina just said. She was right, I was not a lot of fun to be with. Now I know it. I just wasn't dealt a hand of cards that made me somebody who was able to look at the world and say, "Hey, this is one amazing Merry-Go-Round ride … Let's make the best of it while we're still on it!" No, that wasn't me. I was more the kind of person who always felt his emotions were in a strait jacket, who always held back, who couldn't let go, who never knew how to truly love anyone or anything. I can't pin down the cause. That's just the way I was. What cause can ever be pinned down? I was a joyless person who didn't mind if the people around him were joyless too. That's why my two wives prior to Georgina flew the coop. The first one left me a note saying:

Charles, you're not a bad man. But I'm leaving you because I can't stand the idea of another year, another month, another day of such a bland life. I'm not a cow grazing in a field looking for nothing but a little grass to eat. No, I want more. I want to climb mountains, I want to swim across oceans, I want to shake the stars in the sky. Good-bye Charles. I wish you all the best.

Sincerely, Micheline

P.S. You can keep the furniture and anything else you want. I'll be living with my mother until I find a place of my own. As we don't have any children – thank Zeus – you won't have to give me alimony or any such thing. You've been good to me. I want to be good to you. I'll get by. The divorce will be easy.

I kept this note. I never showed it to anybody, but I never threw it away. She was right, but I was not able to change. However, I wasn't able to live without the company of a woman either. My second marriage lasted two years. It ended a little messier than the first because I found out that Sonia had been having an affair with her ex-husband for over a year. I had never heard of such a thing before … but it was true. She divorced Richard in 1970, married me in 1971, and in 1972 started seeing him again. He was a traveling salesman for women's cosmetics – soap, hair dye, and whatnot – and was able to set his own hours, and hence was free to see her quite often. We had no kids, I worked, Sonia was a mouse to play while the cat was away. But, in retrospect, how could I blame her? I wasn't a good lover. I didn't make her laugh. I didn't give her what she wanted. I honestly don't know why she married me in the first place. I guess she saw me as the opposite of Richard, to wit, a man with a restricted sexual appetite who would not be sneaking out on her all the time. She had divorced Richard because he was seeing other women. When she became his "other woman", she forgave him his sins and gave me the boot.

Georgina was different, different because of her ultra-conservative upbringing. It wasn't in her nature to want to climb mountains and shake stars. She just wanted someone with whom she could share a modest home and raise children. She didn't want fireworks. She didn't want a passion that would carry her to the moon. We had what you might call a symbiosis, not one that was particularly beneficial to anybody, but one in which neither party incurred injury from the other. Neither sucked the other's blood. Neither tipped over the other's boat. But neither brought much joy to the other's monotony. At the time I thought Georgina and I were right for each other. Now I think we were perhaps both wrong for each other. We each could have used a spark, a royal kick in the butt, someone to show the way to a little taste of heaven on earth. Like I said before, there is no God, there is no *other* world of justice, brotherly love, and champagne and strawberries for everybody. There is no second chance. It's now or never for those walking above me. It's too late for me and my neighbors.

When I look back on it all, I'd say my life was far more tragic than Lucie's. Hers was short, yes. But at least she lived before she died.

CHAPTER 14

Let me tell you why I don't like Christmas. First of all, as children, my brothers and I didn't receive presents. Santa Claus never came to our house. He came to our neighbours' houses, but not ours. My parents believe Jesus is the son of God and all that, but they don't think Jesus's birthday should be celebrated with a decorated pine tree, mistletoe, eggnog, gifts wrapped in bright paper, and an old man with a fat tummy, red suit, and a bunch of reindeer who flies around in the sky and pops down chimneys with a bag-full of goodies for all the world's nice boys and girls. No, no. That's not the way the world works. There are no goodies in this life. No Santa Clauses in this world. No bearded old men to compete with Jesus and Jehovah. The only Gift Giver is the Great God All-Mighty Himself and all his presents are reserved for the "next life". So, the only thing my parents want to do on Christmas is to get together as an extended family, sing a few canticles, say a couple of prayers, read scriptures, and share a meal.

Basically. that's what they do every Sunday. For me and my husband it's about as exciting as a seven-day-old donut. But we do it ... for the "family" ... for the twins. The truth is, I *want to love* my family. But, as is so often the case, families are complicated; families contort the chord of "love" with multifarious twists, turns, and knots; families are not born to make the ocean of life smooth sailing.

When I stopped believing in my parents' god and their version of Christianity, I became more or less a *persona non grata* in the family. I went away to the university. The cherry on top of the cake was when I got pregnant out of wedlock. I married Philippe two months before the twins were born, essentially to keep the whole building from blowing up. The first few years my husband and I had our own Christmases. When the girls got older, I decided they should have the experience of spending Christmas with Grandma, Grandpa, their aunts, uncles and cousins. I made passable peace with my parents and started inviting everybody to our house on the 25th. I've done it for four years now. I can't say it's a lot of fun, but it *is* interesting. It's rather like visiting a mental hospital. I suspect it's the same way with most families. Philippe and I do have our own party on the 24th with the twins and a visit from Santa Claus.

Four years ago, my parents were nice enough to rent the house to us at a very reasonable price. Did that mean they had forgiven me my truckload of sins? No, not really. But I think they thought that getting me back into my childhood home might provide a steady stream of memories about God, Jesus, the Holy Ghost, and the sacred "family circle", and that this might bring me back into the fold … and bring my atheist husband along with me. Actually, Philippe is more of a pantheist than an atheist. He thinks God is in insects, flowers, loaves of bread, rocks, tomatoes, tigers, and yellow tennis balls. Good God is everywhere! Even in the plastic Christmas tree he puts up every year because he believes cutting down real trees for decoration is a capital crime that should be punishable by castration! … Anyway, after these years in the house, I'm no closer to coming back to the religion than my husband is to becoming a monotheist. But I do appreciate living here and I thank my parents often for their generosity.

When I think about it, maybe I shouldn't really say *"I don't like Christmas"*. Let's just say that it always turns out to be a rather *odd* occasion. This will be the first time Georgina comes. When Charles was alive, they had their own Christmases at their apartment in Pully with some relatives from his side of the family. This will also be the first time in ages for my younger brother, Frederic. He dropped out of the religion – and the family – shortly after me. He's three years my junior, and is the total opposite of my older brother. His path has been about as rocky and full of holes as any can be in the quagmire of our so-called "modern civilization". He dove deeply into a sea of drugs, dropped out of school, couldn't hold a job, played in a busted heavy metal band, had a few run-ins with the police, and ended up in a psychiatric hospital totally estranged from everybody in the family except me. We've stayed close through it all. He's out of the mental institution now and says he's off drugs. After years of great suffering, he finally seems to be doing much better. He even has a girlfriend that he met in the hospital. Last week when he called, I invited him for the Christmas Day party. He hesitated, but finally accepted saying he would take out all his piercings (lips, nose, ears, above the eyes, etc.) and wear a long-sleeve turtleneck sweater to hide all his tattoos. He even said he might cut his hair.

My older brother and his wife and four children have come every year. They're religious fanatics to the bone, but their femurs and tibias aren't quite as hard as my parents'. Harold is not a bad guy by any means, but we have absolutely nothing in common except the fact that we both popped out of the same uterus and in all likelihood the same sperm bank provided the other half of our chromosomes. His wife is a bit overbearing sometimes, but their two older children get along really well with Isabelle and Julie. It's good for the twins to have some cousins.

I have an older sister who died at childbirth. I often wonder, had she lived, if her life would have changed anything in the family. I wouldn't have been in the middle. Maybe I wouldn't have been the peacemaker. As it is, all her death did was reinforce my parents' belief in God. They have said three things that I can never forget: first, that the Lord decided at the last minute that Pauline had another mission in heaven that was more urgent than her mission on earth; second, that God decided Pauline was already a pure spirit and did not need to be tested with a life on earth; and third, that Pauline's death was a test to their faith in God Almighty and they had passed the test with flying colours!

Can you believe such a view of this world? Everything, absolutely everything makes sense. A tsunami that kills a quarter of a million people and destroys everything in its path one nice spring day is just part of God's lovely plan. Who knows? Maybe God was pissed off because some girl like me got pregnant out of wedlock!

In any case, it is impossible for me to share my parents' view of the world. So, what do I do? I try to salvage what I can to "keep the family together" – whatever that means. I don't have the guts or the desire to cut the cords and fly away. Sometimes I'd like to. Maybe I should have years ago. Maybe one day I will. But for now, when Christmas rolls around, I play hostess to every family member who wants to come. It's not easy, but it makes life interesting and it gives the twins "a family".

Last night I counted: there are fifteen people coming for the day. I don't mind the work and preparation. It keeps my mind occupied. I try to remember that these get-togethers have a purpose.

And today *is* special with Georgina and my younger brother coming. I don't know how long it's been since Frederic has talked to my parents. I have told them he'll be here and that he wants to smoke the peace pipe. I suspect my mother will make some kind of effort to reunite with him. How? I don't know. But I think she'll at least try to extend a hand to him and to his girlfriend. My father is a different story. A story nobody really knows. A story that hangs over the family like a huge storm cloud waiting to drop hail and shoot thunder and lightning. I think I know more of the story than anybody else, primarily because I'm not afraid to look into the hearts of men, even if I know I'll find ugliness and perversion. If there's a hell, it's here on earth ...

Everything is ready. They're all coming at noon. I've made a big buffet so I don't have to be in the kitchen all the time. I did most of it last night. Isabelle and Julie were my most able and willing assistants. To have such wonderful daughters almost makes me want to believe in a heaven ... or at least in a family. I wonder if I'll still be saying that eight or ten years from now.

Before I greet the guests, I'll just tell you how the oldest male, the family patriarch, the top of the totem pole – my father – will comport himself today. We are all creatures of habit, and his behaviour has not changed since I've been old enough to observe it. As soon as he arrives, he will look for an excuse to leave. He will take off his coat, say hello, and sit down in a chair in silence. He will make very little eye contact with anybody, but me in particular. He will accept a glass of white wine, but before he has finished it, he will slowly rise and tersely explain that he must excuse himself for a few minutes because he forgot to do something. My parents live just a hundred meters down the street and his business is next to their house, so it's easy for him to have an excuse to absent himself. He will return about a half an hour later, just in time to eat the meal. He will never explain where he has been and what he has "had" to do. He will eat in relative silence. He will look directly at nobody. And as soon as dessert is finished, he will disappear again for "work" or a nap. You would think he'd be happy to see his six grandchildren together. You might think he would be happy to see Harold and me (and this time his estranged son). But no, he will show no joy in being with any of us. He will give one impression: he wishes he didn't have to come to these events.

Is this because he thinks we shouldn't be celebrating anything? Is it because he believes the only thing to celebrate in this world is God? I don't believe so. I think it's for a completely different reason. If you want to know the truth, I don't think it has anything to do with God. Of course he plays the game, puts on the face, wears the mask of a man who loves and worships an almighty Being. But what Being? Certainly not the God of brotherly love that Jesus talked about. Certainly not a God that loves his children. Certainly not a God of light. Maybe there is a God of darkness. Ah, here's a question for thinking people: Is there more light or darkness in the universe? There are lots of suns and stars out there giving off lots of light … But think of all the darkness in between those stars. If one could stand outside the cosmos and look at it, would it be a mass of light or obscurity? (Why my mind goes to places like this is beyond me … But it does. So I live with it. Just like I live with my father …)

My brother's wife makes up for the absence of a patriarch at the party. She wants to be the matriarch. She wants to dominate every conversation. She is as sure as Plato that she knows how God's world functions. (Was

Plato really sure of anything?) In her case, the only two things she's ever read in her life are the Bible and the Reader's Digest, but as far as she is concerned, they're the only sources of knowledge a brain needs. My husband Philippe can't stand listening to her, but he rarely intervenes. I actually kind of like to hear her talk. To be ridiculous without knowing is a blessing.

I'm really glad Georgina is coming. The more I get to know her, the more I like her and the more I'm fascinated by her life. She's actually one of the most honest people I know. She admits everything, she hides nothing. She never tries to make excuses for herself. She has had a boring life and she admits it. She's fat and she accepts it. She is starting to see the world in a different light and she shows it. She loves her visits to the cemetery. They are not part of a baleful morbidity; to the contrary, she makes the cemetery come to *life* ... she makes the cemetery feel like Beethoven's 'Ode to Joy' is rolling over the tombstones. She and Frederic should add a little spice to the soup. My mother is usually pleasant on these occasions. I am curious to see how she will get on with my dear disheveled chaotic little brother.

The doorbell just rang. It's five minutes past noon. The hostess will now rise and greet her first guests.

CHAPTER 15

Jana was a perfect hostess. She is so considerate and good to everybody. The food was delicious. Of course I ate too much. But what other sensual pleasures do I have? I hadn't seen her brother Harold for a long time. I had forgotten how overbearing his wife could be. I hadn't seen Frederic for ages either. His girlfriend is almost as fat as I am! But she seems nice and treats him well. Obviously, he needs someone with a kind simple heart. I think she has one.

It was my brother that really surprised me. I don't remember him being as removed and fidgety as he was yesterday. He looked like he didn't want to be there. Not ten minutes after he and Anna arrived, he said he had to quickly go do some work at his office. Who has to do work on Christmas Day? Especially someone who has his own business selling orthopedic equipment ... He came back a half an hour later, just in time to eat. He hardly said a word during the meal. I noticed my niece watching him a lot. After the meal we sang a few songs and then had dessert.

He mouthed the words and hardly touched his crème brulée. Dessert done, he left and never came back. His wife seemed − or pretended − to take no notice, as if his behavior was normal. But it wasn't normal at all. He's the oldest male in the family. His daughter made a huge effort to provide a nice meal and a pleasant day. He shouldn't be leaving all the time. Unless he's sick or something. Maybe he is sick. I don't know if I had just forgotten what he was like, or if he has changed. It's true that I haven't seen him for a few years. What struck me the most was that he hardly communicated with his beautiful twin grand-daughters. After he left, Isabelle said, "Why did Grandpa leave so early? Doesn't he like Christmas?" Only Anna, his wife, ventured a response saying he was tired and needed to rest.

While Jana and I were doing the dishes, I asked her if anything was wrong with Robert. "Your brother − my father − ," she said, "has been acting like this since I was eight years old. I haven't felt his eyes on me tenderly for as long as I can remember." That's all she said. I must say I was shocked. Even Charles had moments of tenderness with our children. Can it be the silly religion that makes a man so cold? Can God put ice in a man's undergarments? When I tried to pursue the subject with Jana, she said we'd talk about it another time. I pushed her no further.

Of all the people there (other than Jana), Frederic touched me the most. He seemed as fragile as a fine teacup. I watched his eyes rest periodically on everybody in the room, like he was actually trying to look into everybody's *soul*, like he cared about *everybody*. He reminded me of

Dostoyevsky's character in "The Idiot", Myshkin, who was just too *good* and too *innocent* for this world. How can you care about every person, every creature? Thousands – millions – of living beings are suffering and dying every second. A person who truly cares about everybody and every creature has a choice: either go crazy or find a way to black out the suffering. Is that why Frederic fell into drugs and a mental hospital? Has his whole life been an effort to try to find a way to cope with tragedy. Or has it been all about his family and the mess of the religion that he, after Jana, stopped believing in? Is it guilt? Confusion? The loss of a foundation for living? Or is it a little of all these things, all mixed up in his cute head? I hadn't seen him for probably fifteen years. And there he was, meek as a fawn, holding the chubby hand of his girlfriend, smiling at everybody, as if he were Jesus Christ himself resurrected in Vevey, Switzerland for a Christmas dinner at Jana and Philippe's residence, my old home; the home where Robert and I were raised with a view of this world that grabbed hold of our youthful heads, like a clamp on a metal pipe about to be sawn in two.

I thought of the people in the room who had left the religion for good: Jana, Frederic, and myself. Each of our roads has been very different. I thought of those who were still clutching the iron rod of Christian fundamentalism: Robert, Anna, Harold, and his ridiculous know-it-all wife. They are all very different people. What is it that makes a person turn out to be what he or she is? Can we ever know? Why is my brother so cold and distant? Why is Jana so warm and kind? Why has Frederic ended up looking like a twenty-first century Jesus? Why is his girlfriend as fat as I am at age twenty-something? Why is Jana's husband Philippe a discrete man with a happy disposition? Why did Harold marry a bitch? Why is Anna seemingly at peace with getting old? Why can't her husband warm up? Why are the twins the happiest kittens on earth? Why am I, at age sixty-seven, asking all these questions? Shouldn't I have given up trying to understand people a long time ago?

I had intended to make a quick visit to the cemetery after I got home. I thought I'd chat with Lucie and then say good night to Charles. The clock said ten past nine. Instead of putting my coat back on and heading out the door, I plopped myself down in my chair. I stared at the dead TV. Suddenly my head said, *"The dead can wait ... The dead can wait ... The dead can wait ..."* Now where did that thought come from? Then the same head said, *"The living can wait ... The living can wait ... The living can wait ..."* Then it said *"No they can't ... No they can't ... No they can't ..."* Then, *"Wait for what, Georgina? ... Wait for what? ... What are you waiting for, Georgina?"*

I closed my eyes and my head started doing a slow spin. The next thing I knew today was here. And now today is almost tomorrow.

CHAPTER 16

I don't know if I'll ever tell Georgina the truth about my life and that I killed myself. She could find out on her own if she did some research because my story did get in the local newspapers a year or so after I died. But she'd never think of doing that. How could she? I didn't make the news because I killed myself. No, that happens to people every day. My case made the news because of what some people thought my stepfather had done to me. But he didn't do anything to me. We did things to each other.

I jumped off the suicide bridge in Lausanne, the Pont Bessières. It's the Swiss version of the Golden Gate Bridge. Both are magnets for people looking for a way out of their world. The San Francisco jumpers land on water. In Lausanne you hit a road a hundred feet under the bridge. The unlucky ones hit a car or a pedestrian. Unlucky for the car or the pedestrian, that is. I got nothing but blacktop.

I've tried to keep Georgina happy. When I first saw

that I actually had a chance to influence her life, I jumped to it. (Funny … same word … *jump* – *jump* to your death … *jump* to the opportunity to help someone out a little.) I fear that if I tell Georgina what really happened to me it could throw her for a loop that she might never recover from. That's what happens to people like us. I say "us" meaning all the sensitive types who feel the earth's suffering under our feet and in our veins so much of the time. Of course, our vision of the suffering of others is tied to our own suffering. In fact, it's probably pretty hard to separate the two: when *I* suffer, I feel the suffering of *others* more acutely; when I see others suffer, it's easy to link *their* suffering to *my own* suffering. It's a circle that slowly builds into a whirlwind. Then suddenly, the whirlwind becomes a tornado. Later, just when you think the wind might be dying down, something else happens and *WHAM!* You get thrown up in the sky again. Then another thing happens. *WHAM!* The next thing you know you're on the railing of the Pont Bessières.

Before I ended my life, I did have moments when I thought I could live a reasonably normal life and carve out a decent existence with enough joy to make me want to live on into old age. But then, *BOOM!* The hole in my gut would grow like a wild tumour and I knew I wouldn't make it past twenty-five. It turned out that I couldn't make it past twenty.

At first, I thought that killing myself would be a quick decision, but the more I considered it, the more I realized it was going to be a choice that I had been slowly making my entire life. For me to finally do it, so many things had to have happened, so many thoughts had to have zigzagged through my head, so many emotions had to have run through my body, such an intricate chain of events had to have come together. No, killing myself was not a split-second decision. It was the explosion at the end of a very long fuse. I am not against suicide. If it's the only way, it's the only way. I don't think it's on the cards for Georgina. In any case, if I can, I'd like to be a positive piece in her puzzle. I'd like to be a link in her chain of living, not dying.

Another thing I've been thinking about – as I feel the worms making their way through my cheap casket – is how stupid it is for me (or anybody else) to think that I (they) will ever be able to pin down the precise "who" or "what" was responsible for my death. Everybody wanted an answer – my parents, my friends, the judge, the newspapers, the public. *Why? Why did she do it? WHY? WHO CAUSED IT? WHAT CAUSED IT?* Now I know: there is *no* answer to the question. Nobody knows WHY … I … DID … IT. Georgina was right yesterday after the Christmas dinner when she was thinking about the reasons for everybody being who they were … THERE ARE NO ANSWERS. Everything is too complex. Everything. Causality goes back to the beginning of time and the more I think about it, the more I am convinced there was no beginning of time. How could there have been? Something coming from nothing makes no sense! I think the whole bag of marbles has always been. It just gets shaken and the marbles keep moving and it's all constantly changing. But in the end, it's all tied together and connected. What people do is find reasons and explanations for everything – why their lives are the way they are, why the earth turns and the rain falls, why I killed myself, why Hitler did what he did, why the price of coffee is going up, why Bill and Diana split up, why Sally got cancer, why there are termites in the basement, why Terry didn't call, why their spouse was unfaithful, why their team lost, why the poor are poor and the rich are rich, why Africa is so far behind in technology, why technology took so long, why slavery, why some skins are pinkish-beige and others reddish-black, why I am turning to dust ... Of course, one can always give answers to all of these questions. Nothing is easier. "Oh yes, Lucie killed herself because first her stepfather ... then she and her boyfriend ... and then ..." But even if all that were true, that's not WHY I killed myself. Another girl could have had a similar situation and *not* killed herself. There is always more. Much more. And why did this and that happen with the stepfather and why did this and that happen with the boyfriend? What infinity of causes went into all that? Why was my boyfriend not the perfect person for me? There will always be another question to ask. There will always be a question preceding the last question and the question before that and the question before that. Courts of law, like people everywhere, always find a moment when they stop digging and say who or what *is responsible*. But they are never right. Never. They always simplify things. Their conclusions are always premature. They never get to the bottom because there is no bottom! That's what I've learned as I rot away in this grave! There are always reasons for the reasons. Reasons concerning the make-up of the brain, reasons concerning the treatment one received as a child, reasons concerning the responses to stimuli of the millions of cells in the body. Of course, the world's courts of law have to make *somebody* responsible. The victim, the victim's family, friends, the world ... Everybody wants a clear-cut *guilty* creature. But *who* or *what set of circumstances* were responsible for the one deemed responsible? And who or what before that? And on and on and on. Jesus understood this when he said "Judge not lest ye be judged". But since then, nobody has understood it. At least nobody with any power. Of course, some criminals should be taken off the streets. Nobody would disagree with that. But not because they are "guilty", but for the simple reason that they are a menace to society, like termites or rattlesnakes, or scorpions, or dangerous dogs. Maybe the real criminals are those who think they know the answers. They perpetuate the dumbness and the misunderstanding. Until people admit that everything goes back forever and ever, they will never begin to "understand".

I died at age twenty and I've been dead for twenty years. What have I begun to understand? This: I don't blame, I observe. I observe the complexity. Should I blame God for passing out the minds and bodies that he did? Should I blame Mother Nature? Evolution? Should I blame human hormones? Chromosomes? Weak brains? Strong brains? Sexually obsessed brains? Violent brains? Aesthetic brains? Or, ladies and gentlemen of the jury, should I blame the unthinkable ... *NOTHING?* Or maybe

I should say *EVERYTHING*.

If we want to have a chance see this world *correctly*, there is another thing we must do: we must eliminate, once and for all, the idea of *free will*. As long as we believe in free will, we will always believe in "responsibility", we will always be living a lie. Only when we realize there is *no* free will does it become possible to accept the horror, the suffering, the tragedy, the suicides, the love, the beauty, the seasons, the flowers, the snow, the floods, the famine. It is not God's will. Or man's will. It is not destiny. Destiny is as much a myth as free will. Man is not some unique free species outside of *nature*. Man is nature. If there's a God, He's nature. Everything is nature. Nothing is free. Nothing is destined. Not man, not God ... nothing. Nothing happens because of this or that. Everything happens because – as the chief in "Little Big Man" says– *that's the way things are*, because of infinity, an infinity of causes, an infinity of effects, the same infinity that put our little world where it is in the first place. The same infinity that has always been.

This is what I've learned. The living are simply too blunt to see it. This might be the greatest tragedy of all. Or – who knows? – maybe the greatest blessing.

CHAPTER 17

Wow. What a mouthful. I like this neighbour of mine, this Lucie! I used to be a little jealous of her because of all the time Georgina spent standing over her tomb. Not anymore. Now I'm glad. Georgina certainly doesn't have a lot of time left. Lucie is trying to help her make the best of it ... something I didn't do.

When I listen to Lucie, I often try to imagine her last moments alive, when she climbed up on the railing of that bridge. Was she able to stand up? Did she keep her balance and throw her arms up to the sky and make a final gesture to the world? Did she actually bend her knees and jump? Or did she just throw a leg over the railing and, once her body was on the other side, her hands loosened their grip and she fell? Did she dangle for a few seconds before letting go? Did she suddenly have second thoughts and try to pull herself back up? How was she dressed? Did anybody try to stop her? Did she do it in the early morning? Late at night? At high noon under a warm sun?

Or was it rainy or foggy?

I compare her death to mine. I died because I got old. Eighty-three. I never would have had the guts to kill myself. Nor did I want to. I died like I lived. Calmly, resignedly, silently. I didn't fight it. I didn't want to revolutionize my stable boring life. I let it run its course, like a flat stream inching its way to a large river. The river of death.

The last year, until I finally went to the hospital, Georgina was extremely good to me. She dressed me, fed me, helped me walk to and from the toilet. She always kept a good temper. She always had time for me. Actually, I guess she didn't have much else to do, other than watch TV. We eventually bought a second TV for the bedroom.

Mine was a slow steady deterioration. One by one my vital organs started wearing out. I was like a car – first the brakes wear down, then the tyres, the motor, the heater, and finally the windows won't go up any more and the radio stops working. My kidneys went, then the liver, lungs, prostate, brain and heart. I died at three in the morning like an old car in the middle of the Sahara Desert on a clear starry night. Georgina had been with me at the hospital that evening, but had gone home to sleep. The nurses on the floor were dozing off and all was quiet. I didn't say a word. I died.

Yes, I died like I had lived … alone. Of course I had had three wives, Georgina being the only one that lasted. Yes, she and I had had two children. But I never really came out of my shell. I never really let my hair down and let my engines roar. I was a *Swiss* Swiss, raised in the shadow of

Calvin and Zwingli, fearing a God I didn't even believe in, fearing the state, fearing what people thought of me, fearing the police, fearing for the safety of my children, fearing I might lose my wife. I suspect the only thing I didn't fear was death. Why? Because I never really cared about life. I never treasured it. I never saw its beauty, its mystery, its magic ... even its insanity. I never felt the raw wonderment that anything exists at all. I lived my whole life wearing thick dark glasses. You could say I never made love to life. I never let life make love to me ... But I think Lucie did.

CHAPTER 18

There are mice in there. Lots of them. Even in winter.
When there's no snow on the ground they come out. The
snow rarely stays for more than a couple of days. When it
melts, I go back to the cemetery.

It's getting across the street that's risky. There are
quite a lot of cars. I often cross with the fat lady in the
morning. She lives above us. We're on the ground floor.
They wouldn't let me out for a long time. How long? I
have no idea. Finally, my meowing got worse and started
annoying them. They opened the door. Now they've put in
some special window that I can get in and out of. I come
and go as I please. Life is much better.

I probably cleaned out the mice in the garden behind
the building in a month or two. I don't know if I killed
them all or if they suddenly got smart and moved away. In
any case, when there were no more here, I started going
across the street to the cemetery. It's a cat heaven. I'm
pretty much guaranteed a mouse or two a day. I still set

some of them on the doormat for the family. But somebody always scoops them up and throws them away.

I don't know for sure what it is that I like about mice. But when I see or smell one, I know I have to have it. When I pounce and get it between my teeth, there is a quick rush of heat that runs through my body. I usually immediately bite into its neck without killing it. I like to keep it alive for a while and feel its warm body and blood. Sometimes I let it free and then bat it around with my paws. I give it one last chance to play *Hide and Seek*. But I almost always win. Rarely does one get away once I've had it in my mouth. There are birds that come, too. I even got a pigeon the other day. There is a big difference between the soft fur of a mouse and the dry silky feathers of a bird. I prefer mice, but every now and then I enjoy the challenge of catching something else.

CHAPTER 19

I don't really want to accuse anybody of anything, but I remember my father told me to never lock the door to the bathroom or to my room. He said it was dangerous, that I could get myself locked in. In summer, when we would go to the swimming pool, he would never play with my sister and me, that is, he would never throw us up in the air like other fathers did with their children. He would sit on the grass and watch us get in and out of the water. One thing that really got me wondering was that when the twins were babies and my mother saw Philippe helping me change their diapers, she told me one day that she wouldn't let my father ... her husband ... change my diapers because she was afraid he would be tempted by Satan to do things he shouldn't do. I never forgot that. Did she, because of her religion, think that all men were born evil and that this life was just a test to see if they could resist temptation? Is that how she viewed her own husband? Is that how he viewed himself? Did she think

God had put these urges into his body and that He – God – was testing her own husband? Didn't she realize that most men don't desire young children? Babies! Did my mother think all men fantasized about their own daughters? I do remember that he came into the bathroom seemingly pretending he didn't know that I was in there, and that when I got a little older and started locking the door, he became angry. I recall an incident when I was eighteen or nineteen and I came home one night at two o'clock in the morning. I had snuck quietly into bed, and he suddenly burst into my room, turned on the light, and jerked the covers off me. I was naked. I remember his eyes, like bullets burning my flesh.

And then there was my younger brother, Frederic. A few years ago, before he went into the mental hospital, he told me that he feared that he couldn't resist young children, and that he might do something with one sometime. He said that when he felt the things he felt inside, there was no holding him back. He even told me he had urges toward elderly women.

Was this a genetic thing? Was Satan real? Did some human beings simply have uncontrollable urges. I was probably sixteen when I truly started questioning why any human being did what he or she did. Both good behaviour and bad behaviour became a mystery to me.

When Frederic reached puberty, he told me he really feared he couldn't control himself. At Christmas, when we were alone for a moment, he thanked me for having helped getting him committed to an institution before he destroyed himself and somebody else. It made me so happy to see him out now, with a girlfriend, and on the road to being able to have a life.

My father has always been out, free to roam the world. He has had a wife for nearly forty years. He has two sons and a daughter. He has a business that functions smoothly. He says his prayers and goes to church. He is respected in the community. Why has he never looked at me or treated me with simple fatherly tenderness and love?

CHAPTER 20

When I went to the cemetery yesterday, the cat from downstairs ran across the street in front of me. It raced to the gate and went inside. When I was visiting with Charles, it came up and slithered between my legs. I stooped down and petted it. It's a beautiful creature with the markings of a tiger and yellow-brown marbles for eyes. It ran off, but later came back while I was chatting with Lucie. This time it had a mouse between its jaws and looked like it owned the world. It strutted past me, then ambled across Lucie's tomb. The mouse fell from its mouth and I watched the cat walk away. I knelt down and stared at the mouse lying dead on its side. It reminded me of a miniature toy buffalo, except that its neck was punctured and slightly bleeding. Its body was arched and its short legs were pointed back as if it were running across a prairie. I had a paper handkerchief in my coat pocket with which I picked it up. I might have tried to bury it next to Lucie, but the ground was hard and I had no shovel or sharp object with which to dig.

Lucie, what do you think I should do with it?

Disposing of the dead has always been a problem. Can you imagine how many creatures pass from life to death on this earth every single day? And not only on dry land, but also in the oceans, lakes, and rivers. I'm sure there are far more that die in water than on land. I wonder what happens to them?

Maybe they get eaten by other sea animals, I don't know. I've never thought about it.

I have. There must be billions of them that die every day. And nobody cares. At least nobody I've ever known.

Oh Lucie.

Georgina, I know you're a caring person. But it's impossible to care about everything. No mortal mind has the time or the space in the heart or head to care about everything. Even a heart as big as the moon could only care about a tiny fraction of all the creatures in the world. Just think about how millions of mice will die today.

I know. I look at this beautiful little body and I cringe.

Georgina, that's part of the reason I died. I was young and just couldn't accept all the suffering and death. For all that, you are wiser than I was.

No, I don't think so Lucie. I thought so much about my own situation that I didn't have time to worry about the rest of the world …

I stood there for I don't know how long. Lucie didn't say anything else. The cat had disappeared. I still had the mouse in the handkerchief in my hand. I tried to think that if I were the mouse, what would I want done with my body? If I had a heart attack and died in a heap on Lucie's tomb and a mouse found me, what would I want that mouse to do? I wondered if all the dead should simply be food for the living. Isn't that generally how the world works?

I finally set the mouse under the big tree next to General Guisan's tomb and went home.

CHAPTER 21

I love Georgina. She's a wonderful woman. It's been a week since the episode with the mouse. That day I went silent for a hundred reasons. She always seems to understand. Since that visit the ground seems to be getting warmer and our conversations have been getting longer. And interestingly (for me at least) we're starting to get closer to each other. How close? I've always wondered how close people can or should get? Can you get *too close* to someone? Is it impossible to get truly *close* to anybody? One thing is certain: she now spends a lot more time with me than she does with Charles. But just because you spend a lot of time with somebody doesn't mean you're *close* to that person. In any case, I've started to tell her a few more things about my life. She seems ready for a good dose of truth …

I told her about my mother leaving my father not long after I came into the world. Usually it's the other way around, that is, if anybody packs up and takes a hike with an infant in the house, it's usually the male. Actually, he did leave, but not because he wanted to. She's the one who fell in love with someone else. How many women with a young child even have time to fall in love with another man? I think I was about sixteen months old when she met my stepfather. She was pushing me in my stroller down by the lakeside park. He was sitting on a bench reading Camus's book "La Peste". My mother was (is?) a great reader. She asked if the other half of the bench was free and sat down next to him. I made a few noises and she lifted me out of the stroller and planted me between herself and the man she would eventually fall in love with and end up raising me with. I don't know if she fell in love right then and there, but I do know we sat there for a long while. She told me the whole story when I was old enough to listen. The man did a few *Gilly-gillies* with me and a conversation started between them, and, for all I know, it's still going on …

My mother had a lot of guts to tell my father she loved another man when she had two small children. Maybe "guts" is the wrong word. But that was my mother. She was bold. She would say things like, "What are people supposed to do in this world? Marriage is supposed to be sacred, but of course it isn't. It can easily happen that after you get married you meet someone that you like better – or in a much different way – than your spouse. So, when that happens, what should you do? Most people stay with their spouses so as not to rock the boat. Is that the right thing to do?"

My mother was not a follower of the herd. She also

could not kill a fly. Or a mouse, for that matter. She believed flies and mice had as much right to life as she did. She also believed she had the right to love whomever she wanted whenever she wanted.

At the time my mother met my stepfather, my sister had just started kindergarten. That meant that she and I were free every morning until my sister finished at 11h30. My real father was an engineer and worked ten hours a day. He would leave at seven-thirty every morning and not come home before seven at night. It was early summer when my mother met my stepfather and their paths crossed frequently in that park by the lake. Their conversations became longer and more intimate. William was two years younger than my mother and had never been married. One morning she invited him to our apartment for coffee. Later, he invited us to his house where she first heard him play the piano. He was a music teacher. Eventually, he set all his music lessons for the afternoon and my mother started leaving me with an elderly neighbour whose husband had died and who was happy to have some company in the morning. The rest is history. Of course I was too young to remember any of this. My mother explained it all the day she told me that William wasn't my real father. When I started telling the story to Georgina a couple of days ago, I suddenly put myself in my mother's shoes. It was a curious moment ...

So, what happened? How did your father find out?

No, he never "found out". She told him. She told him one night after my sister and I were in bed. She told him she was leaving him for another man. Evidently my father didn't say a word. They were at the kitchen table. He listened with eyes of steel. My mother said it looked like his body was frozen. When she finished talking, he rose from the table, walked to the hall, grabbed his coat, and hurried out the door. She had expected a big fight, maybe some yelling and screaming and tears. But no, the man who fathered me didn't say a word. He only came back to get his things when he knew she wouldn't be home. I don't even know is he ever saw me again until my funeral. Within a month, he had quit his job and moved to Australia. My mother, sister, and I quickly moved out of the apartment and into William's house.

So, you were too young to remember any of this. And your sister, does she have any memories?

Not really. She said she had a vague memory of our father.

And he never came to visit you while you were growing up?

No, he didn't. I think that's why he went to Australia. He wanted to be as far away as possible. My mother said he was not the kind of man who could be happy just seeing his children on weekends. Like I said, I don't think he came back to Switzerland until my funeral. He was a very sensitive man and, according to my mother, had had to completely cut the cord to keep from going crazy. Looking back, I think I got my sensitivity from him.

But he came to your funeral?

When Georgina said this, my spine went cold. The idea of my father and William in the same church for my funeral … but it happened. William was on the front row. My father was in the back of the church, alone.

How did he know you had died?

My mother told him. She found one of his old friends in Lausanne who had his phone number in Melbourne. She called him.

Oh, Lucie. I'm so sorry.

Don't be. At least don't be sorrier than for that mouse on my tombstone last week ...

And then I went silent.

CHAPTER 22

This morning at eight-thirty Georgina called and said she wanted to talk to me. I invited her for tea. She was in Vevey within the hour. The twins were at school. We were alone in the house. I hadn't seen her since Christmas.

When she walked in the door, she had a look on her face that I hadn't seen before. I wouldn't go so far as to say that she looked self-confident, but she definitely wasn't the submissive, reserved aunt that I am used to seeing.

... It's my friend Lucie I want to talk to you about. For the last few days now, she has been opening up to me about her life.

It was a short life, wasn't it?

Yes, she died when she was twenty years old.

Do you know why or how she died?

In part, yes. Jana, Lucie ... told me ... that ... she killed herself. The words did not come out smoothly. *First she told me that her father ... was not her ... real father, then ... a few days later ...* Here, she paused for a long moment. I invited her to come into the kitchen for tea. As I was preparing it, she told me that Lucie had jumped off the Pont Bessières bridge in Lausanne.

Did she tell you why?

As soon as I said that, I realized what a silly question it was ...

No, not really. She just told me that her mother fell in love with another man when she was two years old and that her father went to Australia and she never saw him again and has no memory of him. She didn't find out that her stepfather – the man her mother fell in love with – wasn't her real father until she was fourteen hers old. She knows that her real father came to her funeral. But as for the rest, Lucie said it was too complicated to explain then. She said maybe we'd get into it when spring came. Of course, I didn't know what spring had to do with anything, but she acted quite serious. I guess there's a time for everything. One thing she did say was that when her mother told her father that she was in love with another man, her father didn't say one single word. Can you imagine that? Most men would start throwing things across the room, shouting obscenities, and maybe even taking a punch or two at the woman or the wall. But her father just sat in the chair like an ice statue and stared into space. When she finished, he got up and left the house for good.

I let Georgina talk. She obviously needed to. All I said was ...

So, Lucie has no memory of her real father?

No, none. But like I said, he did come to her funeral.

Nothing more was said about Lucie. It's interesting how sometimes we fully listen to what a person is saying, sometimes we half listen, and sometimes we don't listen at all. As Georgina spoke and we drank our tea, I went through all three stages. Little by little Lucie's story started interweaving with thoughts of my own life. Even though it was an amazing – even shocking – story, it slowly gave way to *me* … me thinking about my own life and my own story. As Georgina spoke, for what must have been at least five minutes, I nodded a lot and said "yes" and "oh Georgina" a few times, but by the end – I'll be honest – I was only thinking of myself, my father, and my *home*. Of course I cared about Lucie. But the self has to be cared about too.

CHAPTER 23

The fat lady picked up the mouse with her handkerchief and finally put it under a tree. I didn't want it anymore. I wasn't hungry and it was dead so I couldn't play with it anymore. All the mice I bring to the family usually just get thrown down the toilet or tossed in the garbage can. I don't understand why they don't eat them. They eat sheep, cows, pigs, chickens, fish. Why don't they eat mice? Is it because mice live in holes in the ground? Do they think they're dirty or something? Rabbits live in holes in the ground, don't they? They eat them sometimes. They don't know what they're missing. Mice are so much tenderer than a piece of a cow or a sheep. Sometimes they drop pieces of cows in my bowl, but I can hardly chew the stuff. The fish they give me are pretty good though. Once in a while I'll kill a bird and give it to them, but they never eat them either. There's just something about mice that I love. I can't get enough of them. But when I kill one, I'm not always hungry.

CHAPTER 24

This morning Georgina came early. It's getting warmer and the days are getting longer. She brought daffodils. She knows they're my favourite flower. My mother used to plant them in our garden when I was a child in Bern. They signalled the end of winter, like a stop sign saying no more cold and snow. Georgina had been spending a lot more time with Lucie than me, but now I'd say it's about fifty-fifty. And she's changed a little. It's not often that an old person changes. I'm not talking about the body, but the personality. Maybe more the mind than the personality. With age, most people just become more solidly what they are. But not Georgina. Lately, she's been saying things that I never thought would come out of her mouth. She's seeing life differently. Is it Lucie? Maybe. This morning, she told me about Lucie's suicide and she sounded like she wasn't shocked anymore. I couldn't believe it. Instead of being horrified, she gave me the impression that Lucie jumping to her death was, in the end, as normal as rain falling from the sky. It's as if nothing surprises her anymore. She seems to have stopped fighting the world. Here's how our conversation went today:

Hi Charles.

Good morning, Georgina.

I think you might be interested to know some things I've learned about your neighbour Lucie over there.

Sure. Anything to liven up the party ...

We both laughed.

So ... Charles ... at the age of twenty, Lucie became so desperate that she jumped off the Pont Bessières in Lausanne. Do you know when the bridge was built? I didn't. I looked it up. It was finished in 1910. I wondered who the first person to jump from it was ... and why.

Why did Lucie jump off the bridge?

I don't know because I don't have all the pieces to the puzzle. I'm beginning to understand that I'll never have all the pieces of the puzzle. No matter how long I talk to Lucie, no matter how much of her life she reveals, I'll never have the full picture. I'll never have an understanding of the brain she had, the body, the heart, the soul, the toes, the temples, the teeth, the thoughts. I'll never know the stories of all the people she interacted with, the people she became desperate about. Finally, now, in my old age, I'm starting to see that we are always walking and talking on the surface of things. No matter how hard we try, we can never get to the heart of anything. Nothing.

There was silence for a good moment. Was this the Georgina I had lived with for decades? Finally, she broke the quiet ...

When I first started to think this, it frightened me. It made me sad. I started to panic because the idea went against everything I had been taught as a child ... even everything I had been taught as an adult. Everything was supposed to make sense. The whole world was supposed to have a logic. Everything was supposed to be explainable. Every story was supposed to have a beginning, a middle, and an end. Suddenly I realized this was all a bunch of baloney. Yes, talking with Lucie has helped a lot. She has shown me the complexity of things. Jana has too, but in a different way. I don't see the world the way I used to, Charles. Nothing is simple anymore. And it's so complex that I wonder if it's even worth the effort to try to make sense of anything.

I never thought I'd hear you talk like this, Georgina.

I never thought I'd hear myself talk like this.

We both laughed again. I think I can count on one hand the number of times I remember us laughing together in our many decades of life together. We were too serious. Now I know. If death has taught me anything, it's that I should have laughed more. I wanted to kiss Georgina. Maybe she even wanted to kiss me. In any case, I forgot to thank her for the daffodils.

CHAPTER 25

Why *us?* What have we done to deserve this? My family is almost decimated. Twenty dead in the last three weeks. We moved to this cemetery thinking that here, finally, we had found a place to live in peace. Peace? It's been almost a murder a day. All at the paws of one damn cat. And it doesn't even seem hungry half the time. If it ate us to stay alive, I could understand. But it doesn't. Yesterday it killed a sister, ate half of her, then left the rest on some flat stone.

And why the torture, the batting around with the paws before it finally kills? What did we do to deserve such cruelty? We've never hurt a cat in our lives. Never. And it's never a fair fight. It waits, pounces, breaks the neck. There's no competition. No battle. Yet it acts proud, like it just won a damn beauty contest or something.

Yesterday it came within a hair of getting me. I had just stepped out of the hole for a look around. Fortunately, there was some light that bounced off its eyes so I could see it crouching not far away. I made it back home before it could get me.

It's no fun living in terror. We can't leave our hole without fearing for our lives.

CHAPTER 26

I swear, in twenty-four hours we have gone from winter to spring. Yesterday it snowed all morning. But by late afternoon it had all melted. And today, when I went to the cemetery, I didn't even need a coat or a jacket.

For a couple of weeks, I have had the feeling that Lucie was going to get to the story of her suicide. She did. At least part of the story ...

Hi Georgina. I've been waiting for you.

Hi Lucie. There's another mouse on your gravestone, but I haven't seen the cat for a few days.

He's around ...

I pushed the mouse off the stone with the toe of my shoe.

... Did you sleep well?

Recently I've been sleeping well almost every night. I'm making up for those sleepless months after Charles died.

Georgina, part of what I'm going to tell you was in the

newspaper. But newspapers don't tell a hundredth of any story. I don't know why people read newspapers. They always just brush the surface.

I know. I've finally figured that out. But please, go ahead. I think I'm now ready for whatever you have to tell me. I wouldn't have been ready three years ago, or even three months ago, but now I feel like I am.

I know. And the truth is, a few months ago I did not tell you the truth. I made up a story about me falling in love with a boy named David when I was sixteen. I did fall in love, but not with a boy named David ... I said nothing and Lucie continued *... Georgina, when I was sixteen years old, I had become a rather beautiful girl. At least that's what people said, both with their eyes and their mouths. Maybe I should say "woman" instead of "girl". My body was that of a woman, but of course my brain was still somewhat that of a child. My stepfather, William, and I spent a lot of time together in the house. My mother had decided to go back to work. She took a job at the university library and worked from ten to six, Monday through Friday. William gave a few piano lessons each day at the house. I often came home for lunch at noon, whereas my sister didn't. I finished school around three-thirty. My sister rarely came home until about six because she always went to her boyfriend's house. Anyway, you see the situation. William and I were alone together a lot.*

Yes ...

William was what you would call "an aesthete". He loved beauty. He was like the man in the book, "Lolita". He loved music, of course, but he also talked a lot about painting, sculpture, photography, and so on. I'm quite sure that's why my mother fell for him in the first place. In any case, that's why "I" fell for him. He made me feel like the most beautiful creature in the world. At first, I thought nothing of it, thinking he was just a stepfather trying to be nice to his stepdaughter. We always had a pleasant relationship. He was very kind to me and my sister. He also had a sense of humour, and we laughed a lot together. One day after school he was playing the piano and the door to his music room was open. I came and stood at the portal and listened. I don't remember what the music was, but it was lovely and rather simple. Maybe a Beethoven sonata ... No, I think it was the second movement of Mozart's 21st Concerto ... It doesn't matter. Or maybe it does. Anyway, there I was at the door. He sensed my presence and turned. He stopped playing, asked me to come over, and offered to teach me the first few bars. I sat on the bench next to him. I think I told you before that he was younger than my mother and a good-looking man who dressed more like my friends than a forty-year-old. He usually just wore old jeans and a pullover of some kind. To be fair to him, I think the fire was inside me first. Remember, I was sixteen. Puberty was ablaze on all fronts ...

Lucie paused. But not for long.

... So he started showing me the first few notes of the music. Suddenly I lifted my left hand towards the keys. I put it on top of his right hand. He didn't move. A few seconds later my shoulder leaned into his. Was I lonely? Was I a cat in heat for the first time? Did I "love" him? I didn't know. Maybe it was a bit of all three. I hadn't planned anything. It just happened. And, for whatever reason, he did nothing to stop me. Did he love me? Had he and my mother stopped loving each other? Had they stopped making love? They had been together for a dozen or so

years. I really knew nothing about their situation other than that they never fought and always seemed reasonably content. Anyway, we stayed like that – our shoulders touching and my hand on his – for what was probably thirty seconds but seemed like an eternity. Then he turned towards me and put his other hand on the inside of my knee. He was gentle. Our eyes met and we kissed. It was not a passionate kiss, but it was warm and gentle. He was the one who first pulled away. I'll never forget how he looked at me. His eyes froze for a second on my face. They were eyes that must have been full of a thousand emotions: fear, passion, doubt, love, desire, a kind of madness … He then suddenly stood up and, without a word, walked out of the room. I heard him go into the kitchen. I think he poured himself a glass of wine and went outside. I went into my room and shut the door.

Lucie was silent. Of course I wanted to know what happened next. It turns out, there was much more than I had ever imagined. I broke the silence …

Lucie, that's almost a beautiful story.

It "was" a beautiful story. For a moment. For a month. For a year …

Do you want to tell me?

Yes, I want to tell you. I've never told anybody what I just told you. Before I killed myself, I told my friends the dark side. I told them what happened in the end. But the beginning was a fairy tale, a love story outside of time and space and civilization. I never really thought about his age or my age, or even the fact that he was my mother's husband. It was like a dream. I just thought of how his lips felt on mine and how he made me feel so beautiful.

She hesitated, then pursued.

For a few days, neither of us said anything about what had happened. The weekend came and passed normally – me with my friends and he with my mother. Then on Monday I came home at noon for lunch. He had fixed something nice – I can't remember what – and while we were eating there was a moment when our eyes met and it was as if they were locked together with steel tubes. My body suddenly froze, but it was like a frozen fire. Again, I was the instigator; I put my hand out across the table. He took it. We both stood up and I took two steps into his arms. This time we kissed passionately and went into my bedroom and made love. I was a virgin. He was my stepfather.

It was as if Lucie's tomb trembled softly in the earth. Or so I imagined. I also imagined her relief in finally telling somebody how it all happened. Can the dead cry? It didn't matter. I felt like I had a best friend, so I said …

I just want you to know I'm not judging you at all. How could I?

I know, Georgina. Otherwise, I wouldn't be telling you all this.

At that moment, the cat appeared and floated between my legs to a stop. I petted it, waiting for Lucie to say something else. She didn't.

The cat's here, I finally said.

What does it look like?

A brownish grey tiger with yellow stripes and yellow eyes. I picked it up, but it immediately jumped out of my arms and scampered away.

Is it purring?

No, it just ran away.

Well, Georgina, that was the beginning. The first time I fell in love. Maybe the only time really. Did I pick the wrong person? Who is to say? He was tender, gentle, intelligent, and he seemed to appreciate everything about me. Not only my beauty, but my young mind and how I dealt with other people and growing up. Later, when I tried to be with boys my age, it never felt the same. I tried not to love William, but it was impossible. And as you know, unfortunately our civilization looks down on a forty-year-old with a sixteen-year-old, especially when the sixteen-year-old is his wife's daughter.

Yes, Lucie ...

The sun was getting warm and I was overdressed. I took off my coat and looked at the sky. There were a few billowy clouds coming in from the west. Lucie said that was all for today, but for me to be sure to come back tomorrow.

CHAPTER 27

Why do people always want to pick us up and *hold* us? I know some of us like it, but I don't. I don't like the feeling of being stuck inside two hands and a chin. I guess they like the feeling of our fur. But I don't like the feeling of their skin. And sometimes their breath smells bad. And then when they want to hold me on their lap and pet me for a half an hour … Do they think I've got nothing better to do? I'd rather be looking for mice. Or sleeping. But I don't like sleeping on a lap with hands crawling around my back. Granted, some of us do. But we're not all the same. I like sleeping alone, on a chair or in the basement or on an empty bed. We don't think they're all the same. Why do they think we are?

I've started spending a little more time in the apartment because the cemetery isn't much fun anymore. I think there's only one mouse left and it'll never come out of its hole. The other day I waited for what seemed like half the day. I could smell it. I knew it was down there. But it refused to show its face. I need a new hunting ground. And there are too many damn cars in the neighbourhood now. Last week two friends, Floo-Floo and Chester, got hit. Floo-Floo didn't have a chance. A bus hit her. Her body looked like a plate of ketchup and old food. Chester didn't die right away. I found him near the entrance to the cemetery. I tried to get him to move, but he looked at me and shook his head. He died a few minutes later.

Floo-Floo and I had made babies together. Chester and I fought over her. I won, but still had to go see the guy with the green shirt with the smelly office. He knocked me out and when I woke up, I wasn't the same. Part of me was missing. Chester finally got his chance with Floo-Floo.

CHAPTER 28

Georgina and I just had lunch together. I have never seen her so animated. She told me everything Lucie had told her about the beginning of her relationship with her stepfather. I listened, but to be honest, it hurt. Not because I have anything against a sixteen-year-old falling in love with her mother's husband. True love on this earth is so rare; I'm not one who is going to write rules for it. No, that wasn't the problem at all. The problem was comparing Lucie's experience to my own experience. It's amazing how different relationships can be with a mother, father, brother, sister, spouse, etc. Why? We're all so different. So, when Georgina finished telling me Lucie's story, I decided it was time for her to hear a few things about my story with her brother ... my father. Lucie had love with the man who raised her ... all kinds of love ... even the greatest passionate love. I had nothing of the sort. My father never made me feel loved.

Georgina, I appreciate you telling me all this about Lucie. I wonder how many people know the story.

I don't know.

In any case, the same story can be very different depending on who's listening and how it's told.

I told you because I had no one else to tell and I knew your mind would be open to receive it.

As you talked about Lucie, I couldn't help thinking about my own story with the man who raised me ... your brother ... my father. The man who never gave me any love.

I decided to be direct. Georgina did not look surprised. Only sad. I knew she wanted to hear more. I gave it to her.

Your brother never looked at his daughter with soft warm eyes that say, "You're a lovely girl, Jana" or even, "You did well on that test in school". When you described how William looked at Lucie and made her feel so loved and beautiful, that's what made me think about what I have lived. The total opposite. The sad thing is, when I was young, I thought all fathers were like that. It was all I knew. Slowly but surely, I saw other fathers – of my friends – who actually loved their daughters and their daughters knew it. My father never made me feel loved. He never made me feel warm or beautiful. If anything, he made me cold and his eyes looked at me as if I were a danger to him ... It has taken me years to figure it out, but now I think I finally have! And it all goes back to something my mother once said when I was about the same age as Lucie was when she fell in love with her stepfather. At age sixteen I was a young woman. Men were starting to tell me that I was lovely and beautiful. But never my father. I once asked my mother why? She said one sentence that I have l have never forgotten ... "Jana. When you were a baby,

I wouldn't let your father change your diapers because I feared he might do something the Lord didn't want him to do." ... Yes, that was it, my mother was afraid my father would not be able to resist temptation ... with his own daughter. That was the world you and I were raised in. Life was about sin and temptation. Our instincts were evil. My father did not see me as a daughter to be loved, but as a temptation to be avoided. What a tragedy! Today I understand it. My father wasn't an evil man; he was a sick man. Made sick by his view of the world.

I had nothing else to say. I felt relieved to have said what I needed to say ... to somebody. That somebody was my dear aunt Georgina. The longer I lived, the more I appreciated her.

CHAPTER 29

I hadn't had a visit from my wife for three days. Maybe it was four. When she came, I sensed she was walking slowly. I don't think it was because she didn't want to see me. I think it was that she was thinking. We had a conversation that made me feel like she was happy to talk to me. Strange as it may sound, death and time are starting to bring us together. I guess it's often that way, but not always. Sometimes death is a curtain dropped at the end of a bad opera. You just want to forget about what happened. But in my case, death has made me wish I had taken advantage of what I had.

Georgina told me all about Lucie and Jana. Lucie's story so far only goes to when she was sixteen years old. Jana's is up to the present day. I'll be honest, the business about Jana's father didn't surprise me at all. I never had much contact with him, but the few times I saw him, he never showed warmth and love to anybody. Even less than I did. I always wondered what kind of life – including his sex life– he would have had without his religion, without the guilt, sin, and fear. Could he have had "a normal" sex life? What does that mean? I surely didn't have one. I was frustrated as hell, too. I eventually just let my juices dry up and more or less forgot about the whole thing. Georgina and I were cooked chicken after we had the kids. I was getting on in age. And besides, hardly a woman on earth ever showed any interest in me, so I decided I wouldn't show any interest in them. In my case everything kind of happened by default.

Looking at Jana's father from my perspective now, I agree with what she said: the whole thing is sad. That's the only word for it. Maybe sick, too. Sad and sick. No healthy man would "be tempted by the devil" while changing his daughter's diapers. It's amazing Jana turned out as well as she did. My guess is that her intelligence saved her. She was too smart to be sucked into the idiocy of the dogmatism. She didn't – doesn't – see the world in black and white. The fact that she has no ill-will towards her father says it all. It's actually kind of a beautiful thing. She's the only real Christian in the family ... Well, maybe she and Georgina ...

The story of Lucie and her stepfather is a different bag of marbles. It looks like it really was about a man and a young woman who loved each other. I guess the question is whether or not a sixteen-year-old can be considered a "woman". But everybody matures at a different age. The truth is a lot of people *never* mature! They stay infants their whole lives, trading in Santa Claus for God. That's why I hated religions. They keep people down. But like somebody said, maybe people need to be kept down. Maybe they don't have wings to fly. If you can't fly, you walk ... or crawl. Hell, I was kept down pretty much all my life. I never let myself go. I never flew. It wasn't because of religion. It was because of ME. I was shy, introverted. I never wanted to rock the boat. I always combed my hair and kept my shirts ironed. I just wanted to get across the ocean of life with as few waves as possible. I wouldn't have had the *guts* to fall in love with a sixteen-year-old girl. But was the stepfather wrong? Was he the cause of Lucie's suicide? Did he ruin her life? I imagine Georgina will find out about all this later.

We talked longer than usual. She is experiencing things that neither she nor I ever thought she'd experience. She's living, she's feeling, she's searching. Before it's too late. I'm happy for her. Had I given her more love, she might have been one of the happier people on earth.

CHAPTER 30

I feel like a tree with no leaves in a razed forest. Naked.
Alone. I'm the only one left. The cat has killed everyone
but me. Now you might understand why we reproduce so
much. We have to in order to avoid extinction. Nobody
respects us. Nobody appreciates us. But we still want to
live. My only chance is to make a break for it and find
another community of my kind. But it's so dangerous out
there. And it's not only cats. Dogs, birds, people. They all
kill us. Maybe people are the worst. If they're not
murdering us in laboratories, they're poisoning us or
setting ridiculous death traps with pieces of cheese. Talk
about genocide! What have we done to deserve such
treatment? What have we done to hurt anybody? Nothing.
Absolutely nothing. Why can't we be left alone to live in
peace? Like I said before, if they killed us for food, I
wouldn't say much. But they kill out of stupid prejudice
and hate. They kill us for sport. They kill us for what they
call "science". I think I'll make a run for it tonight. There's

a quarter moon. Should be enough light for me to see and be gone.

CHAPTER 31

I'm back again Lucie.

Hi Georgina. How have you been?

Fine. I just had a nice chat with Charles. Jana is coming again for lunch tomorrow. The weather has been most pleasant. Some people don't like spring. But I do.

I always preferred summer. I never liked to wear layers of clothes. I should have been born in Africa.

Were you coquettish Lucie?

Yes and no. People used to tell me I looked good in anything, so after a while I wasn't so concerned about clothes. I bought most of mine in second-hand stores.

Didn't your stepfather buy you things?

Rarely. We had to be so careful. But of course, he gave me presents on my birthday and at Christmas. William and I were always extremely discreet. I would say we probably made love two or three times a week for three years until I was eighteen. We always did it in my room. Never where he and my mother slept. Right after we made love the first time (I was lucky I didn't get pregnant), my mother suggested I start taking the pill. Of course, she didn't know anything about William and I. It was a strange coincidence. Or maybe it wasn't. I was ripe for picking and she could sense it. What she didn't sense was that it was her husband who was getting the fruit. But Georgina, don't think our relationship was just about sex. It was wonderful to make love, but we also talked about everything. We shared a love of beauty and life. Where is it written that a sixteen or seventeen-year-old can't love the world. And besides, I slowly came to realize that William was extremely lonely. In fact, I'd say he was the loneliest person I ever knew. But that was part of what I loved about him. All his loneliness was poured into me. He filled me up. Little by little I realized how much he needed me and truly cared about me. I think he told me things he never told my mother.

Did you feel guilty with regard to your mother?

The truth is, I didn't. And do you know why? There were two reasons. First, William told me their physical relationship had been over for a few years ...

And you believed him?

I had no reason not to. I never saw them kissing or holding hands. I never heard any noises coming out of their bedroom. And I don't think he ever lied to me. He had no reason to. Of course we talked about this a lot. He often said he didn't want to hurt my mother. As I've told you, he was a sensitive man. I would say a truly good man. He was attached to my mother ... as far as I know, he still is ... but their relationship had taken on a brother-sister direction. Their bodies didn't matter to each other anymore. And William's body couldn't be separated from the rest of his being. A dead body was a dead being. He had to share his body with someone he loved or else he would go crazy. He told me that many times. Actually, he had to share his body and his mind or he'd go crazy.

He didn't go crazy then?

Not that I know of.

So neither of you felt guilty with regard to your mother?

William truly loved me. How can you feel guilty about making love to someone you truly love? If you don't love the person, that's a different story. If you're just using her for sex or whatever, okay, feel guilty if you want. But William and I shared so much, and we loved everything about each other.

So, what happened Lucie? You said that you and William made love for three years. Did you stop after that?

Yes, and I'm the one who stopped it, Georgina. When I was eighteen, I met a boy my own age that I really liked. He and I were free to do things openly … in the world. William and I were only free in a bedroom. In a way, the bedroom had begun to feel like a prison. And I'll be honest. I loved to make love and I had tried being with a few other boys. I never told William about them, but I'd sensed he could feel that there might be a crack in our love. I never loved the other boys, and William never tossed jealousy in my face. But then, I met this boy in my school who had cool parents. He loved me and they loved me. I was often invited to dinner. I never told William about him. They had a big house in the country and I started going there on weekends. It wasn't much of a problem because my mother was home weekends, so we – William and I – never did anything on Saturday or Sunday anyway. One Saturday night I slept at Raphael's house and he and I made love. I enjoyed it. It was the first time I had enjoyed it with someone besides William …

I stopped talking. I was starting to recall my mental state back then and how it eventually became hell, the hell that killed me, the hell that sent me into this stinking hole.

Georgina finally broke the silence ...

With Raphael in the picture, things must have begun to get rather complicated.

Yes, they did. I loved William and I loved Raphael. But I couldn't love them both at the same time. It just wasn't in me. I couldn't go from one to the other. Maybe that's easier for a man? But who knows?

Georgina didn't say anything. I kept talking ...

You know, Georgina, you're the first person I've told this whole story to. It's good to have someone to talk with ...

And it's good to be able to hear you. Please go on ...

Raphael was new. William and I were over two years old. It was William who got sacrificed. He could feel it before I told him. He sensed I wasn't as passionate as before. You can't hide things like that, especially from someone like him.

Did you tell him that you loved Raphael?

He got the message.

And what did he do?

Of course he took it like the wonderful man he was. He had no meanness in him. There was something in him similar to what was in my real father when my mother told him about William. He said nothing and went to Australia. William didn't go to Australia, but he began playing music like a madman. Great music was his Australia. When I would come home from school, he would always be in his room beating on the keys as if he was trying to kill them. I remember once when he was playing Tchaikovsky's 1st Piano Concerto. Have you ever heard that, Georgina? Do you know how much human emotion is in that one piece of music? My guess is that Tchaikovsky put half of his life's suffering and joy into that single concerto. Well, William played it like he was playing for the whole world. I'll never forget how I stood outside his door and listened until I couldn't stand it anymore. I went to my room, shut the door, and cried. The music still boomed through the walls. It crashed into my brain. Remember, he was a very lonely man. And when a lonely man loves, he really loves. And when love leaves, he truly suffers. But what could I do? I also loved Raphael. But remember, I still saw William almost every day. We still lived in the same house. We had meals together. At the meals, my mother would ask me about Raphael whom − of course − she knew all about. I was a constant witness to William's suffering.

Did he get over you? Did he find someone else?

He got worse and worse. He drank more and more of his beloved wine. He really did love wine and without my love he must have doubled his daily dose.

Did your mother notice any of this going on?

He hid it as best he could. He'd tell her that he was losing his love for music, that he was having an existential crisis, and that he was starting to feel the reality − he called it the "facticity" − of death. Things like that. But he's not the one who ended up dead! But my mother just thought he was having a middle-age crisis. And I pretended like all my emotions were tied up with Raphael, whom, by the way, my mother adored.

So, tell me, did you feel guilty about William?

Guilty about William? Absolutely. I felt as guilty as if I had dropped the bomb on Hiroshima myself. It killed me to see him like that. I hated to watch him suffer. And don't forget,

Georgina, I loved the man …

Of course, when I said "it *killed me* to see him like that", I didn't mean it literally. I didn't mean that was the only reason I jumped off the Pont Bessière bridge. There's never only one reason. There are lifetimes of reasons for everything everybody does at every instant everywhere all over the whole wide world. Yes, I hated seeing William suffer. But that's only one of the many reasons why I am dead. I continued the story. Georgina was a great listener.

… It turned out that after a year or so with Raphael, my feelings changed. I didn't really love him anymore. I tried to, but the feeling was gone. You can't force love. I realized he and I didn't share the world like William and I did … had. With William, when our love was at a zenith, it felt like we fused into one person. It was never like that with Raphael. He had always been Raphael and I had always been Lucie. With William, even though our love was confined to my bedroom a couple of times a week, we both felt that we shared the whole world together. Maybe I was young, naïve, but I don't think so. It really felt like William and I had fused into one being. And I had taken a sledgehammer and smashed that beautiful creation into a thousand pieces. And I would never be able to put all those pieces back together again!

My tomb shook. Georgina sensed that that was the end of our discussion for the day. I couldn't go on. After a long silence, she said …

Thank you for your friendship, Lucie. I'll go home now.

And then she said something I'll never forget.

Lucie, you have made me feel like a whole person.

And I heard her footsteps as she walked away.

CHAPTER 32

I got as far as a garden across the street from the other entrance to the cemetery. My nose-brain connection told me I had friends over there ... my own kind.

After I got to the other side of the road, I slipped under a fence, and stopped for a second or two to see where I was. That was my fatal mistake. Before I knew what hit me, the killer's teeth were in my neck. It didn't kill me immediately. It played the ridiculous *bat-half-paralyzed-mouse-around-with-paws* game for a few minutes. I cursed the world until I couldn't squeak anymore.

The cat was the colour of milk. So much for the bullshit about black symbolizing the bad guy and white the good guy. The only thing I can say in the cat's favour is that it did eat half of me. The upper half. It must have liked my brains. The next morning a woman came outside with a dustpan and scooped up my backside and tossed it in a smelly garbage bin behind her building. As for the head-torso half, the cat just shit it in the dirt next to some early tulips.

What kind of a world is this? How did a species like mine get created? Were we put on this earth to amuse cats? To be stuck in laboratory cages and fed drug after drug so that some human beings can live a bit longer? Why don't they help *us* live longer? Why do *they* deserve to live longer than we do? Why do they think their lives are worth more than ours?

But I've said it once and I'll say it again ... Nothing gets *created* in this world; everything just happens. No creator would be cruel enough to put me and my family on this earth just to be killed by cats, the same cats that sit on people's laps and get treated like kings ... I know. You don't have to tell me. A lot of these cats don't end up so well either. They starve. They get eaten themselves. They get hit by cars. I think they even used to get their guts taken out to make strings for tennis rackets! What a world!

Yes, ladies and gentlemen. It's a war out there. That's all there is to it. And now I'm out of it. "Dust to dust," as I heard somebody once say. What I sometimes wonder is this ... Are there any caring cats out there? Are there any cats that ever think about our plight? I doubt it. And humans? Do any of them actually care and feel for our existences? A few maybe, but not many. They're too busy believing in their gods, babbling into phones, watching TV, celebrating their so-called "progress", and cheering for the home team in some silly stadium ...

CHAPTER 33

Do people have any idea what eternity means? I remember all this talk about "eternal life". What about "eternal death"? Nobody ever mentions that. But that's the reality: death is forever, not life. Fortunately, I still have Georgina coming around to keep me company. But when she goes, there will be no one. I will be dead forever, forgotten forever. Oh yeah, sure, maybe one of my children might come down from England or Germany to say hello and lay a flower or two on my grave. And if I'm lucky one of my kids' kids will too someday. But it'll end there. I did nothing anybody will remember. But from what I hear, even my famous neighbours – Guisan and Ramuz – get fewer and fewer visitors every year. They'll die out forever, too, one day.

Georgina just told me Lucie's story. It is quite amazing. Of course, we don't know it all yet. What touched me the deepest was when she said William and Lucie had felt like they were *fused* together into one person. I never fused with anything except this goddamned coffin. While I was alive, I was too afraid to fuse with anything or anybody. Afraid of what? That's the question I've been asking myself ... Charles Monnier, what in the hell were you afraid of while you were on this earth? What held you back? What kept your engines from roaring? What kept you from madly kissing the moon and stars and your wife or some other woman?

And now I've thought about it. The answer is as simple as a recipe for a glass of water: I always thought life and people had a purpose. I always thought other people knew what they were doing, but that I didn't. I always thought that I was missing out on something. I was always afraid that other people were looking at me and thinking I was inferior and some kind of a loser. But now I know ... We're all losers. The only winners are the ones who understand this. Now I know ... Existence has no reason to be. Life has no purpose outside of the purpose this or that creature gives it. Only when one knows this can one truly kiss the earth. Only when one knows this can one truly love and live life. Only when one knows this can one truly love another person. Only when one knows this can one truly love and respect anything. When meaning and value come from outside of you – from a religion or a political party or a cultural belief system – it is never *you*. It is always an imitation. You are always riding on someone else's back. You are never on your own two feet. You're always worried about what other people are doing and what other people will think.

Of course, such phony reasons and purposes allow all

us weak sheep to get through life. Of course, religions and cultures and moralities help people stumble down a semi-smooth path of life to their graves. But there is never an *I* that creates its own road. The *I* is always part of a *they*. *I* must do what *they* do, or else *I* am not a *good* person. *They* know the truth about life, so *I* must follow *them*. *I* must do what *they* do or *I* will go to hell. *I* must do what *they* do or *they* won't like *me*. This has been the human battle cry. "Give me something or somebody to follow and give it to me quick! If not, I am a lost sheep!"

I, Charles Monnier, learned too late. Even though I didn't believe in the Christian god, I was still always tied in the chains of civilization. I was always afraid of what other people were thinking about me. I never flew on my own.

When Georgina told me about William and Lucie, I couldn't help thinking that maybe *they* had lived something *real* … something that was really *them* and not just society's way of telling them how to love. I wondered if they really and truly had loved. But having never been there, it's hard for me to know.

CHAPTER 34

Jana and I finally had lunch together again today. It was supposed to have happened last week, but one of her daughters was sick. Julie, I think it was. But before meeting her at the tearoom on the other side of the cemetery, I stopped to say hello to Charles and Lucie. Neither one was in a very talkative mood. Charles seemed somewhat depressed, but I didn't ask him why. I figured he has the right to be depressed every now and then. It's curious how I sense he's changing, how he's slowly opening up all the windows he kept closed all his life. But today I let him be.

Lucie and I talked about where her mother and William are now. The last time we had conversed she said something like, "As far as I know they're still together". But that was all. Today I asked her if she was sure they were still alive and if she knew where they were. She just said that she hadn't had a visit from them for years, but that didn't necessarily mean they were dead or separated or had changed continents. She repeated that after she died, they had moved to Lugano. Then she clammed up a little and I didn't push her. I said I'd be back tomorrow.

But today, it's Jana's story that has my head rolling. Maybe I should say my brother's story. It's amazing how stories get so intertwined!

Since she told me about her father's lack of love, I hardly feel like I have a brother anymore. It feels like he was never alive. What is a brother, anyway? You get born a few years apart of the same mother and father. You get raised under the same roof with the same rules and principles for living. You get old enough to leave the nest. Some do, some don't. Some go far away, some stay close. Some cut the umbilical cord completely. Some never let go. Some stay straddled in between.

My brother Robert stayed much closer to home than I did. And he stayed in the religion. We lost what we had in common. What have we shared or talked about in the last fifty years? Nothing really. We have observed each other at a few family get-togethers, I more than he, I imagine. Then Jana tells me her story and how he made her life difficult. Was I hearing the story of "my brother"? Could she not have been talking about any cold unloving character that you might read about in a newspaper or a novel? I don't know my brother and he surely doesn't know me. Does Jana know her father? Does he know his daughter? People can live in the same house for years and years and still be strangers. Our family is proof ...

One thing that fascinates me is how Anna, his wife, has dealt with it all for all these years – the woman with whom he shares a bed, the woman who gave birth to his three children! Jana says her mother has always been saved by her religion ... her God. Christian metaphysics to the rescue! God fills in all the holes in one's life. It's an interesting panacea! Thank God for God! And my sister-in-law – dear Anna – is sure that her daughter Jana is the one she should pray for because she no longer believes "in God". It's Jana who needs help! Jana who is hell-bound! Anna and her husband will walk hand in hand through the pearly gates because Robert is a "member" of the church. Robert worships "God". Robert repents for his sins. Jana is the sinner. Jana is the bad part of the mix! Can you imagine such nonsense! It makes me want to jump off the Pont Bessières myself. Jana, beautiful Jana, who has never hurt a fly in her life. Jana, who is the most loving mother and devoted wife. Jana who has a mind so open that she doesn't *blame* her father for anything, but tries to understand him, help him, and reach out to him. Jana, who is as kind as any of Jesus's apostles. Jana the evil one? Jana the sinner? Jana the one with a ticket to Hades because she has the brains not to believe in a silly religion founded by a quack prophet? Come on! O God Almighty, stop all this nonsense! Please, stop it! Once and for all!

Do I care about my brother? Of course I do. But I care more about Jana. Robert has made Jana's life difficult. It's not the other way around. Jana has tried to understand. And what has he done? Made her feel like a useless piece of human meat.

Jana and I talked for at least two hours. The more I looked at her face, the more I thought how strong she was.

How strong and how beautiful! She didn't blame her father. She didn't accuse him. She didn't feel vindictive. But I know she has suffered so. What girl wouldn't eventually suffer living with a father so devoid of love? It almost would have been better if he had he died when she was an infant.

Is it too late for Jana? Is it too late to get a dose of paternal love? Probably. Not because of her, but because of Robert. But why can't he see any of that glorious light his Holy Black Book talks about. Why doesn't God or the Holy Spirit whisper in his ear and explain how he has been unkind to his own daughter? Why?... I'll tell you why. Because there is no god. And there is no holy ghost. There isn't even an unholy ghost.

CHAPTER 35

Like I said, half of me ended up in a green garbage bin. The other half went into the white cat's mouth, got swallowed and digested and eventually shat into a flower garden. Half of me will go up in smoke and the other half will decompose and mix with earth. Reincarnation? If you say so. But I tend to think it's all a bunch of baloney. It all just goes through the great cosmic blender.

CHAPTER 36

Lucie ... Lucie, it's me, Georgina. Lucie, please, I need to talk to you...

There is no answer.

Lucie, you must listen...

There is no answer. Georgina is short of breath. She has dashed as fast as she could to Lucie's tomb. She will talk and Lucie will hear without speaking.

Two weeks ago...I think it was two weeks ago...you told me that your parents...William and your mother...were probably still in Lugano. I think...I think it's not the case, Lucie...I think your father...your stepfather...is here...in Vevey. Lucie, are you listening? Lucie!...Jana was in the Payot bookstore this morning...reading the back cover of a book...I just talked to her on the phone...a man was standing next to her...He said something to her...They started talking...He invited her for a drink...She accepted...She said she didn't know why...She said he was maybe fifty-five...sixty...still a good-looking man...There was something about him that made her think he might be interesting to talk to...They went to the café...He said he was...used to be...a musician...a pianist...and that he had lived in Ticino for many years...not Lugano...but nearby in Ascona....When Jana asked him what he was doing in Vevey, he said his wife had died and he had moved back to be near his daughter.... They talked for a while.... Jana said that talking to him was not like talking to most people... She said he seemed "thick"...that was her word... "thick"... like he had lived many lives...like he had seen around many corners, looked inside a lot of bushes and behind a lot of trees...you know what I mean.... He told her he had basically stopped playing and listening to music and had nearly stopped reading, but he had come to the bookstore because he suddenly had had an urge to talk to somebody... "Reading is conversing"...He said it, not me... But with reading, you usually never meet the person you're talking to...like you and me, Lucie...like...oh, it doesn't matter...Anyway...Lucie...when Jana got up to leave and say goodbye, the man asked her her name.... She told him...Then she asked him.... Lucie, he said it was William....

CHAPTER 37

We're all in this together. We all know a few things about everything and nothing. The longer I'm here the more I tend to think nothing is winning over everything. But maybe we'll talk about that later. For now, I'll just say I might know why Lucie didn't say anything this morning while Georgina was telling her about her stepfather being back in the area. She couldn't talk. It was too much. When things are too much, silence is the only solution. I don't care if it's in life or death, there are moments when the mind can't take any more and it shuts down. Words mean nothing. Life is too much. Death is too much. Who feels this? Who understands it? The most sensitive souls of course. The ones who realize what I have finally come to realize after rotting in this grave for a year. What really matters is outside of so-called "civilization". It seems like the more "civilization" we get, the less people appreciate existence, life, and death. All the gadgets and toys and technological advancements only chew up people's time faster and faster. Nobody takes time to think about being alive. Nobody marvels at existence. People don't feel the miracle of the blood running through their veins. They only marvel at what new car or telephone is on the market, or what new gadget will pour music into their ears.

And do you know what's worst of all? Nobody has time to love ... I can't believe I just said that. Me, Charles Monnier, a walking iceberg while alive, just said, "Nobody has time to love." But that's it. Nobody has time to love this earth and to love it with somebody else.

Georgina ... O my dear Georgina ... I didn't give you your due. I gave you my little finger, but I held back the rest of my body. I gave you a few words, but I never gave you my mind. I slept with you, but I never fused with you. I shared some minutes with you, but we never shared the years ... And those years flew by at the speed of light ... Or should I say at the speed of life and death?

CHAPTER 38

Yes, I knew what Georgina was going to say. But that's neither here nor there. We know what we know. Why we know it is of no real importance. The only thing that matters is what's in the mind. How it, and everything else, got there is forever a mystery. How it works is an even greater mystery. Look at me: when I climbed up on that railing of the Pont Bessières, did it matter what brought me to that state? Did it matter how my mind worked? Was understanding or knowing the mechanics of my head going to change anything? No. The only thing that mattered was whether or not I was going to jump. When the criminal has a gun in his hand, the only thing that matters in that moment is whether or not he pulls the trigger. Why he pulls it or doesn't pull it is useless information, as useless as knowing the chemical formula of water for someone who has jumped off the Golden Gate Bridge.

Yes, William is back. He's ten kilometers away. But I

don't think he'll come to my grave. It's not a matter of courage. No, he has more courage than anybody I ever knew. He had the courage to turn the world upside down. He had the courage to question everything – every value, every truth, every idea of what this world is. That's why I loved him. It's not the only reason, but one of the reasons.

People forget that I *grew up* with William. We spent so much time together – playing, walking, talking, laughing. We didn't have a television. We spent hours in the garden, walking along the lake, hiking in the forest behind Pully. He showed me insects, birds, clouds, tastes, colours, sounds. He taught me to respect everything. He didn't say I had to like everything, but that I should respect all existence. He taught me to see, feel, touch, think, think about my thinking. In the end, he taught me to love. When I became a woman – a young woman, but still a woman – he became the object of my love and I became the object of his. Neither of us planned it that way. But I was the one who lit the match that set our hearts on fire. Did I know what I was doing when I put my hand on his when he was showing me the first few bars of that Mozart concerto? Does one ever know what one is doing?

Of course, the world thinks I was too young and William was too old. But the world doesn't know how we felt. The world doesn't know how we loved. Some women are never old enough to love. Not at sixteen, not at twenty-six. Not at forty-six. Not at sixty-six. Not at a hundred and six. Ditto for men. But I was ready for love. Love didn't kill me. The world killed me …

I don't think William will come to my grave because if

he does, he might explode. He is too sensitive. I can understand that he wanted to move back to this area. It's his home. It's his skin. But he won't make it to my grave. He and my mother couldn't even put my last name on my tombstone. My death came within a hair of being his death. But he didn't kill himself. He decided to live. He decided to live because life was too precious to be cut up any more than it already was. I was dead. He couldn't double the horror.

When we were together, he would often say that he had never imagined that it was possible to feel like we did. He said it felt like we were flying, flying through the depths of an unfamiliar universe, a new universe, a universe with no bounds, with no signs telling you which way to go, no laws telling you how to live, no books telling you what to think, no customs telling you what was right and what was wrong.

He often said he felt like his whole being was going to explode. He used to say that he was a stick of dynamite and I had lit the fuse. Fortunately, the fuse has been long. He hasn't exploded yet!

I'm glad to know he's still alive. He and my mother were off my radar screen for a long time. Death is like life; everything has limits. Ascona was too far away.

One thing I still don't know is whether or not he ever told my mother about what went on between us. I doubt he did. He used to say that any real truth was impossible to explain. Our love was as true as anything on this earth, but if we had tried to explain it to other people, we'd only have been telling lies. All the talk in the world couldn't explain the fusion of our two bodies, our two minds, our two beings. It's the mystery of love that makes love "love". The word can sound so empty sometimes. But like Charles said once, the dead don't really need words anymore! No, I don't think he told her. Had he done so, my guess is she would have been strong enough to accept it. They were no longer romantic. They had become platonic partners. There's nothing wrong with that. My mother had a deep mind. She might have howled and gnashed her teeth for a day or two, but she knew enough about love to know how rare it is. And if she truly loved William, she would have wanted his happiness … True, most people don't truly love. They love what the lover gives them. They love how the lover makes them feel. But do they love the lover if and when the lover's love goes in another direction?

I don't need a visit from William. Georgina is enough. She keeps me in touch with the living. She said she might be bringing Jana by soon. I'm sure she'll tell me how he is.

CHAPTER 39

I was thinking today how interesting it is the way things happen. If Charles hadn't died, he would never have been buried in the Pully cemetery. If he hadn't been buried in the Pully cemetery, I would never have gone to visit him. If I had never gone to visit him, I never would have met Lucie. If I had never met Lucie, I would never have had all these things to talk to Jana about. If my brother Robert hadn't been born and met Anna, I wouldn't have Jana to talk to. If Jana had stayed in the religion, we wouldn't have been able to talk like we do. If I had stayed in the religion, I wouldn't have married Charles. If Charles had stayed with his first wife, he and I never would have got married. If Charles had stayed with his second wife, we never would have got married. If Lucie's mother had stayed with her father, Lucie would never have met William. If William hadn't been reading that book on the bench by the lake in Pully, he and my mother probably would never have met. If he had had to leave one minute before my mother sat down next to him, they probably would never have met. If Robert had not made life difficult for Jana, she might not be the person she is today. If she weren't the person she is today, she wouldn't have been able to understand William when they met for a second time and he started talking about his life with Lucie. If William hadn't been through what he had been through with Lucie, he might not have been able to understand Jana when she started explaining how she had been the object of her father's sick mind. If I hadn't been the aunt she loved, she wouldn't have told me about their conversation. If I had died before Charles died, would any of this have ever happened?

My favourite thing in the world really has become just sitting in my chair with the TV screen as black as night and just letting my mind wander. I tell myself, "Georgina, that little mind of yours can take you to a lot of places. It's as good as an airplane. Maybe even better …"

CHAPTER 40

I was sitting in the post office waiting to pay my bills. It was the end of the month and there was quite a crowd of us all holding numbers in our hands. I suddenly glanced left and the man standing near the door caught my attention. We recognized each other and exchanged a wave of a hand and a smile. It was William. When the chair next to me became free, he came over and sat down. We must have had less than three minutes together before my number came up. Have you ever noticed how many words can be spoken in three minutes? Probably five hundred. Our conversation went like this:

Jana, right?

Yes, and you were William.

Still am as far as I know.

You know, William, I might know more about you than you think I know.

What do you mean?

Well, that first time we met you told me you had lived in

Ascona, that your wife had died, and you had come back to Vevey to be near your daughter. Is your daughter in Pully?

How did you know?

Is she dead?

How did you know?

Is her name Lucie?

How did you ...?

My Aunt Georgina lives in Pully. Her husband died a year ago and is buried in the cemetery there. She visits him regularly. Little by little she started wandering around and one day she discovered Lucie's tomb. It was a mess, so she cleaned it up, brought flowers periodically, and soon she and Lucie became friends.

Friends?

They started talking ...

Talking?

My aunt is an interesting person. I love her to death. Or should I say, "I love her to life"? The living carry the dead inside of them. That makes the dead alive. She and Lucie have become very close. The living can talk. Why not the dead? Georgina talks, Lucie answers ... sometimes. It was the tomb that first got her attention. No last name. Only twenty years of life?

And do you know about how she ...

How she died? Yes. She killed herself. She jumped off the Pont Bessières.

What do you know about me?

From what Georgina has told me about what Lucie has told her, I know many good things about you and Lucie ...

We both looked at the number coming up for our turn.

What's your number?

845. It's up next. And yours?

856.

Jana, Can we meet and talk more? Please.

Of course. When are you free?

Pretty much all the time these days. And you?

How about right after we pay these bills. I have an hour before my girls come home from school.

Okay ... Why don't we meet in the same café where we went the first time we met. Do you remember?

Of course.

Let's say in about twenty minutes.

Okay ...

The number *845* clicked on the post office screen. I paid my bills. I thought back and calculated that William and I had exchanged roughly three hundred words in three or four minutes. Imagine how many words the human race speaks in a day.

CHAPTER 41

Where do they come from? There was none, then there were some, then there was none again, and now … now there's a whole group again. In last night's moonlight I caught three. It could have been a mother, father, and a baby. The baby felt so good in my mouth that I ate most of it even though I wasn't really hungry. The fat lady wasn't there, but I put the two bigger ones on that tombstone she always goes to. I brought over what was left of the baby for good measure. She should find them today.

I had actually stopped going to the cemetery for a while. There were no more mice, so there was no reason to risk my life crossing that road. Then one day – I don't really know why – I saw the fat lady leave the building and decided to follow her. We went through the gate together. She went her way, I went mine. I didn't expect to find anything, but it was only a matter of minutes before my nose filled with that deep rich scent of the living mouse.

Where do they come from?
Does it matter?

CHAPTER 42

Georgina, I met William again on Thursday. We talked for almost an hour. We packed more into that time than most people pack into a year's worth of talking.

I wish I had been there.

Well, you're here. That's enough. What would you like to eat?

I think I'll have the soup and salmon toast.

I will too.

So, what happened with William, Jana? Lucie said she was quite sure he wouldn't come to the cemetery …

We met by chance at the post office. We were both paying bills. Later we met in the same café we had been to before. Of course, I told him what you had told me – about his love affair with Lucie. He couldn't believe that I knew so much, but the truth is, I think he was relieved that somebody knew his story and that he could finally talk about it with someone he seemed to trust. I told him a little about you and me and our having been brought up in a very strict evangelical world, and how we both left it.

Then I told him about Charles's death and how you met Lucie. What I really wanted to know about was his relationship with Lucie and how the three of them lived those three years in the same house ... he and Lucie making love in Lucie's bedroom in the afternoon ... he and Lucie's mother sleeping in bed together every night ... Lucie seemingly maintaining a good relationship with her mother ... and on and on. I couldn't imagine how they juggled all these emotions and survived.

Lucie didn't survive...

And William still feels the pain. There was something about his face and the way he talked that told me that this man had been to the top of Mount Everest and the bottom of Death Valley ... emotionally I mean. I don't think I've ever met anyone as "feeling" as he is. He cares deeply about everyone. Too deeply, I think. He said he's pretty much stopped playing the piano.

We ordered our food. I told Georgina the rest...

He told me that he never could have imagined that such a situation was possible. He said it was only "possible" because he and Lucie loved each other so much. They did absolutely everything to ... how did he say it ...? ... to allow their love the chance to exist. But really, Georgina, can you imagine going to bed at night with the mother of the woman – girl – you made love with during the day and who's sleeping in the next room and all you're thinking about is wanting to wake up the next day to go back to bed with the daughter, but all the while you have the deepest respect for the mother whose daughter is everything for you. Again, he said it was only possible because he and Lucie loved each other so much. Otherwise, it would have blown up in no time.

Three years is a long time...

He said that when you're in love, time together doesn't exist and time apart feels like forever. William said that he absolutely loved everything about Lucie. Can you imagine how rare that is in the world?

I can.

He said it was a situation that was simultaneously absolute heaven and absolute hell. But heaven won ... for a while. One year went by. Two years went by. No one ever knew. William said that the fact that Lucie's mother seemed to have totally lost interest in sex saved him. He said he would drink good wine every night and go to bed early. Lucie's mother would stay up late reading in the living room. She would go to bed when William was asleep. William would wake up while she was still asleep. He would have a cup of coffee and go for a walk by the lake, then come home and play the piano. He said the world felt like Ali Baba's cave because he knew what was awaiting him when Lucie came home from school. Those two hours together, alone, in her room were perfect moments ... until ...

Yes, until their love blew up. I've only heard Lucie's side. What did William say?

He said that little by little he sensed that Lucie was less passionate. At age eighteen she told him she had another boyfriend, a boy at school. How could William argue? How could he object? He couldn't. He didn't. He let her go. But he suffered and she knew it. He told me he didn't know how many times he thought of harming himself. He would hear Lucie come home after school "with her friend" and he watched them go into her room and close the door. Sometimes on weekends the boy stayed the night. Lucie's mother adored him ... Raphael was his name ... But she never knew what was going on in William's mind. First, he had had to hide all his joy, and now he hid all his suffering …

Did he say why Lucie jumped off the bridge?

When I brought up the subject, he briefly said that he honestly didn't know. Then he clammed up and stopped talking. He stared at me for a moment, then eventually he went into a kind of a trance and stared past me. Finally, he dug a hand into a pocket, put a ten-franc bill on the table, politely thanked me for my time, and then got up and left.

How strange?

Georgina, is anything strange when you're dealing with life and death?

I don't know. Is anything not strange?

Our food came. We didn't talk much while we ate. The words "love" and "life" came up a few times. As I recall, nothing else was said about death.

CHAPTER 43

Both Jana and I are wearing light clothes. The afternoon sky is cloudless. We walk slowly towards Lucie's tomb. There is no mangled mouse on her tombstone.

Lucie, Jana and I are here.

Hi Georgina. Hello Jana. How are you?

Fine.

Fine.

So, you have met William, Jana?

Yes, twice. He looks to be in very good health.

Is he happy?

I can't really say.

Did he talk about my mother?

A little bit, when he talked about you.

If you see him again, ask him how she lived the last few years of her life.

I will.

Is he still a good-looking man?

Very much so, Lucie. And very kind. I can see why you were in love with him.

Does he have his hair?

Yes.

Is he fat?

No.

What did you talk about?

Mostly about his love for you.

Did he talk about my love for him?

Yes, and he explained how the flame diminished after two years when you fell in love with the boy at your school.

Raphael. Raphael and William were not the same. I stopped loving Raphael after a few months. I think I never stopped loving William. I thought I did, but I realized I didn't. Sometimes I wonder if I ever loved Raphael.

There are different kinds of love.

I'm not so sure. Not in my case anyway.

William said he loved everything about you.

That's what I mean. That's love. There are no holes.

Did you feel the same way about him?

Yes. The first two years. Then my mind took me elsewhere, I'm not really sure why...

Lucie, can you tell us why you climbed up on the railing of that bridge? I asked William and he said he couldn't tell me why.

Yes, that I can do that. I can tell you why I climbed up on that railing ... but I can't tell you why I jumped. I might have even slipped.

What do you mean?

I mean that I know the kinds of things that were in my mind that eventually led me to that bridge. All that was a long story ... you could almost say "a life story". But what I can't tell you is what happened in the nanosecond when I suddenly passed from the railing to the air. People think I "decided" to jump. I wouldn't say that's true. I "decided" to take myself to that bridge. I "decided" to climb up on that railing. But the moment — the millionth of a second — when I "decided" to end my life, was NOT what I would call a decision. There was a bonfire in my brain. My head was like the center of the sun. To call the moment I jumped to my death "a decision" is just not correct. Looking back one can always invent and "see" some kind of movie of one's life. But one can never "see" the moment one is living.

No one speaks for a moment. Jana's and my fingers touch, then entwine. Finally, Jana says,

Lucie, what kinds of things had been going on in your head that led you to the Pont Bessières?

First, you must understand that in our — your — civilization it is not easy to love. The world's rules often make love very difficult, if not impossible. Jews aren't supposed to love Arabs, Mormons aren't supposed to love Catholics, men aren't supposed to love men, women aren't supposed to love women, married women aren't supposed to love men other than their husbands, a husband is not supposed to love a woman that is not his wife, teachers aren't supposed to love their students, stepfathers aren't supposed to love stepdaughters... and on and on and on... Can you imagine that William and I were never able to share our love with anyone? No one knew about it. Who could we trust with such a secret? Can you imagine carrying that secret for more than two years? Just before I died, I did tell a friend about everything. But it was too late.

Too late for what?

Too late to repair the damage that had been done to my love

with William. You must understand that when I started seeing Raphael, it was such a relief to be able to go places with him, tell friends about him, kiss him in public...all that. William and I had been living in box with no air holes. Eventually I started suffocating. I couldn't stand not being "free". I climbed out of the box and started my relation with Raphael... And I watched William suffer.

If your love with William had been open, do you think you would have jumped off that bridge?

One never knows. Life only happens the way it happens. "If" questions don't make a lot of sense. But the answer is probably no.

Up until now Jana and I have both been staring down at Lucie's tomb. Jana suddenly takes a step back cranes her neck towards the sky. She lets go of my hand. Lucie goes on...

When I was with Raphael, William never blamed me. He never cursed me. He never asked me to come back to him. But I knew how he suffered. Then, a few months later, when I realized I didn't love Raphael anymore, it was his – Raphael's– turn to be miserable. First, I had watched William. Now I was watching Raphael. He, unlike William, constantly begged me to stay with him. He told me he couldn't go on living. He got drunk and banged his head against walls. I thought everything was my fault. I felt like all my "love" had only brought suffering. I was torn with guilt in all directions. And I started feeling guilty with regard to my mother. It all became unbearable. But so did the fact that I knew I still loved William...

You must have felt like you needed three hearts.

Three hearts. Three brains. Three lives ... But I only had one. That's the catch. At age twenty, I wasn't able to juggle everything. I wasn't able to take hold of that one life and keep it alive...

Silence again. Jana and I wait for Lucie to speak.

I'll tell you one thing ... William and I split, but he never left me. He was always in me. Once he got inside me, he never ceased to be a part of me. That's what love is. I carried William in my being until the exact moment I died. Everything: his face, his words, his body, his breath. He's still in me as I slowly turn to dust. We are rotting together. Decomposing into eternity. A few hundred more years should do it ... Don't worry. Now I look life and death square in the face. I don't kid myself about anything anymore. I've seen it. I know what happens. The dead rot and disappear. There is not a trace of billions and billions of creatures, men and women included. Man's ridiculously limited notion of "world history" doesn't include or know 99.999% of what happens on this planet. And it's been going on a lot longer than any archaeologist's shovel will tell you.

O Lucie...

No need for "O Lucie". Lucie is fine, fine where she is. Georgina ... Jana ... I just want you to promise me one thing.

Of course.

What is it, Lucie?

Promise me you will never feel guilty again about anything you do. Guilt is the most destructive emotion on earth. The more I think about it, the more I think that it was guilt that got me up on that railing. I felt guilty about William, guilty about Raphael, guilty about my mother, guilty about myself ... I thought everything going on around me was my fault. And had I really done anything "wrong"? Had I sinned against any god or man? Had I sinned against myself? All I had done was … love. Should one turn one's back on love? I hadn't been cruel to anyone. I had loved people. First William, then Raphael. I had loved my mother all along. And in spite of all this love, my heart was beating a hole in my chest. My brain was on fire. Why? Because I felt guilty. It's that simple. But I never should have. I never should have felt any of it. Everything I had done, I had done because I thought it was the right thing to do. I had never tried to hurt anyone. I'm quite sure that you, Georgina, and you, Jana, are like me. You always do what you think is right in whatever circumstances you are in. But in spite of this, my guess is that you still let guilt chew at your guts, too. Don't. Stop now. Don't let yourselves be haunted again by feelings of guilt or sin. "Sin" is a word that means nothing. Sin against whom or what? There is no god to sin against. There are only human laws about right and wrong. And they differ all over the world. Yes, you can "sin" against your "tradition", but sinning against a tradition is not sinning against God. People think tradition is divine. It is not. It is human. Human through and through. And what are we humans? I've said it once and I'll say it again. We are not what we think we are. Now I know. Humans – especially in our great Judeo-Christian tradition – create a perfect god with a perfect mind and perfect love and perfect "freedom" to be and do. And then these humans compare themselves to this perfect being to whom they have attributed all these perfect qualities. This is their great injurious mistake. Humans are not godlike. If anything, they are catlike, cloudlike, beelike, sunlike. They are as much a part of "nature" as cats, bees, suns, and clouds. Cats don't "sin" when they kill mice. They do what they "have to do". They do what they are. And humans are the same. William knew this. He tried to teach me. I just wasn't quite old enough to understand. Now I do and I love him all the more. Tell him so, Jana, if you see him again.

I will.

And promise me you will try to banish guilt from your world. It killed me. Life should be the only thing that kills...

But Lucie, Jana said, *isn't guilt part of life?*

And there was no answer.

CHAPTER 44

georgina
yes charles
tomorrow is easter isn't it
yes it is
i never liked easter even though my mother's name was ester
i did when i was a little girl because sometimes i got a new
dress
really
rarely but sometimes
yellow
yellow or white   the colors of the resurrection
tulips get resurrected not people
not when the bulb gets dug up and thrown away
right   but put the bulb in the ground and it grows   put the
person in the ground and it rots
i'm glad there's still part of you
yes   but it's getting smaller every day
what a world

georgina don't come tomorrow   at least don't come to me   i
couldn't take it   whoever invented this resurrection business
should be shot
   oh charles
   you know what i mean
   yes of course dear   in any case jana has invited me to dinner
at their house
   that's good   i'm sure you'll have a good time
   i must be going   i'll put these flowers down   goodbye dear
   goodbye georgina

CHAPTER 45

youreearly

iwokeuparoundfourthismorningandcouldntgetbacktosleep

wellimgladyoucame

howwasyoureasterlucie

ihateeaster

sodoescharles

everybodyherehateseaster

icanimagine

howdidyouspendthedayyesterdaygeorgina

janainvitedmetoherhouseitwasanicewarmdayshemadeanice
mealandthenwhilesheandiweredoingthedishesthegirlsandphilip
pehadaneasteregghuntinthegarden

didthegirlsgetnewdresses

yesbeautifulyellowdressesthesametheybothworethem

theymusthavebeenascuteaskittens

yestheyweretheyresuchlovelygirlslucietheressomethingineedto
tellyouimnotsurehowyoulltakeitbutimusttellyou

ofcourseyoucantellmelikeitoldyouthelasttimewetalkedilookeve rythinginthefacenow

wellwhilejanaandiwerealoneinthekitchenwecouldhearphilip
peandthegirlsshoutingandrunningaboutinthegardenshetoldmeso
methingthathappenedlastweekshesawwilliamagaintheymetatthe
marketinthemorningthegirlswereawayforthedayonsomeschoolex
cursionsheinvitedhimtothehouseforlunchshemadeasmallsimplem
ealbutforoncetheyhadalotoftimetotalklucieareyoulistening

yes

shesaidtheytalkedfortwohoursshesaidshehadneverfeltsocloset
oanybodyinherlifeshesaidyoudontplanthesethingstheyjusthappens
hesaidshefeltlikeherbodywasweightlesslikeshewasfloatingbutshe
wasntshewasinherchaironhersideofthetabletheyhadhadalittlewi
nebutnotmuchahalfabottlemaybeshesaidoneofwilliamshandswas
layingnexttohiswineglasssuddenlyshereachedoutacrossthetablea
ndputherhandonhisshesaiditremindedherofwhatyousaidabout th
emomentyoufellfromthebridgeitjusthappenedtherewasnotimefor
adecisionshesaiditfeltliketheirhandswereonelikeitwasthemostnat
uralthingintheworldhisfingersdidntmoveandthenandthenlucielu
cielucieareyoulisteningluciepleasesaysomethinglucielucieforgodss
akesaysomething

Lucie's tomb is silent.

JON FERGUSON

Jon Ferguson was born in October 1949 in Oakland, California, into a devout Christian family, much like his favorite philosopher, Friedrich Nietzsche. In fact, as a child, church services were held in the family living room. At age 17, his passion for sport was almost usurped by a keenness to save the world when he enrolled at the Mormon-owned Brigham Young University. Little by little, though, he realized that if Jesus couldn't do it, neither could he. His faith in divinity began to crumble. Ferguson hopped on a plane in 1973 and by chance ended up in Nyon, Switzerland where he was soon playing basketball in the top Swiss league, becoming a key player in what fans consider to have been the golden age. As a coach, he has won more games than any coach in Swiss basketball history, but he likes to remind people that he lost more than everyone else as well...

He has written over twenty novels and a book on Nietzsche, *Nietzsche for Breakfast* and a book on the history of Swiss basketball, *Of Hoops and Men*. For twenty-five years he also wrote a bi-weekly column in the Lausanne newspaper called "Ainsi Parla Schmaltz". His novel *Farley's Jewel* (Cinco Puntos Press, 1998) won a Barnes & Noble "Discover Great New Writers of America" prize.

Find out more at
www.jonfergusonbooks.com